THE CRUSADER

THE CRUSADER
BLUE EYES AT NIGHT
JP WILDER

EDGE WEAVER LLC

The Crusader

Edge Weaver Realms is an imprint of Edge Weaver LLC

Previously published as two books, The Crusader and Blue Eyes at Night.

Book Design: Marie Pitrat

Kindle ISBN: 978-1-964406-86-2

Paperback ISBN: 978-1-964406-79-4

Published in the United States of America

Edge Weaver LLC
19360 Rinaldi #681
Porter Ranch, CA 91326-1607

CONTENTS

THE CRUSADER
JP WILDER

EDGE WEAVER LLC

CONTENTS

CHAPTER 1
DARK MEN

Through no fault of my own, I found myself surrounded by dangerous men—the Dark Men, as we called ourselves. These were not men in glittering mail and polished hauberks, but murderous rangers—assassins that slit throats and feathered arrows through the enemy's eye. Oh, to be sure, I had heard the clarion call of The God and the offer made by the archbishop to find Absolution wielding sword and axe against the heathen.

Like so many others, I had packed my kit, saddled the family charger—old Swayback, as the tired stallion had come to be called—and bid my family's manor in the pitifully small town of Neder, farewell. I threw in my lot with the Duke

Lethan of Greenshire. He was, after all, my family's liege. The duke forayed south toward redemption and glory at the behest of our King.

We would spill blood so our King might receive his own Absolution.

So, yes, I had set the course that eventually led me there, half-submerged in oily mud and watching a little-used trail for signs of the heathen, so that I might spring upon him and cut him down. But I took no responsibility for this skulking and subterfuge and ... and yes, murder.

I had read the Three Covenants, as laid down by The God, through his archbishop. Written within that treatise, there had been no reference to activities or horrors such as this—only ramblings of Honor and Conversion and Redemption. The Holy Land rightfully belonged to The God and we were going to get it for him, purged of the filth of the heathen. And for this glorious task, we would find Honor—so important to the standing of knights and lords and kings—convert more souls for the glory of The God and find our own Redemption. The damn scribbling had said nothing whatsoever about blood and destruction. Nor did it say anything of murder. I realize now it had been scrawled by an egotistic madman.

It is no place for a knight, mind you—there in the muck with the vermin and worms and worse. But after two years of savagery, I had found that the common understanding of war was woefully inadequate. Honor is a thing not defined by your actions, but by your survival. If you survive and—praise to The God—emerge victorious, you may set the standards of Honor yourself. It is not combat on a flat plain against an evenly matched opponent or striking only an armed foe or charging lancers that ring together like a silvery bell. Nor is it laying down one's cloak, so that a lady's dainty toes remain clean and dry, saved from the horrors of a city's rain pool. It is all clear to me now how foolish I was back in Neder. But there I was, nonetheless, about to make mayhem upon the heathen.

My epiphany was meaningless.

Inadvertently, I sighed aloud at my folly. Sound, as you know, carries in the darkness. It slithered through the woods, around trees and through the silence of the night.

"Shhh," hissed a voice from my right—nearly silent, and sounding like nothing more than a leaf falling to earth. Rayfe, I realized.

He was the best of us—a master of killing who moved like a ghost. The heathen had a nickname for him: Darkstalker. He lived up to the name. And he was no lord to boot—a commoner from the raunchy bowels of Bannon's splendid capital Bannonshire, the Silver City. Still, we followed him like he was a king.

No one killed like Rayfe. No one moved like Rayfe.

I lowered my head and swallowed a yawn. It had been two days . . . two days of traipsing through the woods and marshes around Clurak, keeping to the low ground, wading through rivers and muck, crawling about like lizards or rats, before we had come to this point. Here, by way of this path, the heathens' messenger was sure to traverse to find the army of the Il' Aruk. The path was the only exit from the besieged city which wouldn't be watched—at least not by any sane person. No army would infiltrate the impenetrable fens.

Only it would be watched—by Rayfe, me and the rest of the Dark Men. For we knew—or rather, Rayfe knew—that the heathen did not fear the hardships imposed by the bog. So, there we were. Watching. Waiting. Our job: to ensure that the Il' Aruk did not get word and thus, send his army to break the coming siege.

If things went well and the Holy City fell, then the end of this cursed Crusade was at hand. Before long I'd be on the next cog back to Greenshire and the waiting arms of a flock of waiting maids.

Ah! The ladies of the Greenshire Keep court. I can see them now, spinning and dancing around the duke's ballroom, glittering crystals weaved into blonde tresses and dark locks alike, flashing eyes and smiles that turn the hearts of all the court lords to mush. Ah, yes. And me a war hero—or at least that's the history I'd write. Those court dandies didn't stand a chance. All those scars crisscrossing my chest and neck and face would surely serve to earn a few puckered kisses.

That was the way of being a hero. I'd seen it when the Second Crusade had returned home—victorious from driving the heathen from the Holy City the first time, assured of their Redemption and wearing their Honor on their arms and faces and chests—and telling stories of battlefield glory and deeds of daring-do. Now it would be my turn. At least, all this killing could be good for something, even if it meant only a few soft kisses in darkened corridors and random dalliances in the castle pantry.

"Psst . . ." The sound drew me once again from my visions. I peered through the darkness and saw the void in the dark that was Rayfe. I felt the icy rage in his stare. Incompetence made him crazy and he drove us like animals. Training. Practicing. Killing. At night, when we were not stalking the enemy we stole upon the peasants of this cursed land and slid blades into throats or between ribs, to determine if our skills of stealth were honed enough. What did we care? They were heathens, after all. And so, when we did go into battle, it was with cruel efficiency that we scaled the heathens' walls or slipped beneath their waterways, to murder them with darkened blades and silent crossbows.

I lowered myself down, hunkering deeper behind the thick brush, and peered ahead at the trail. The pathway was difficult to see. Almost invisible in the day. In the night—as it happened to be then—it would take a master to follow its track. If, indeed, a messenger did come this way, he or she—for the heathen had the temerity to send the fairer sex into the bloody business of war—would be a master and no easy mark. It was best I kept my wits about me.

Rayfe must have known something was coming, which is why he signaled me to be on my guard. Within moments, the night seemed to shift before me, almost imperceptibly. If I had not been on a heightened alert, I would never have seen it. But as it was, I was prepared.

Or so, I told myself.

The signal would come soon—a whipper-whistle that signaled the opening of bloodshed. As soon as we knew—as soon as *he* knew—what we were up against, the high-pitched screech would signal the attack. My heart raced and my breath came in short gasps. It was always so, before combat. One must fight to control one's nerves. And I did. I focused, pushed down the urge to flee—or rush forward in mad abandon—and calmed my breathing.

Inhale. Exhale. Slowly and deeply. Inhale and exhale. My heart calmed. My deliberately slow breathing forced the stillness upon me. I called upon my experience and my training to be patient.

Another killing. Another murder. Just another day in the life of a Crusader.

At that thought, an unwelcome pang of sadness rifled through me.

It was not for Honor that I joined the Dark Men. It was not even for the pride of calling myself the best or one of the most feared men in the Holy Land. Though I take no pride in it, I had joined the Dark Men as a matter of necessity. You see, it was about survival. Upon my first combat in this Crusade, I had witnessed the slaughter that occurs on the field of Honor. It is a bath of blood and entrails. Ranks and echelons of men, cut down like rows of wheat. Blood flowing freely over the battlefield, grass slick with their death-excrement, air filled with their pain-filled squealing and the stench of spilled bowels. Few survived unscathed and the fear that came with marching like some construct toward certain death, pin-cushioned by raining arrows or sliced to pieces by walls of scimitar-wielding savages or burned to a cinder by heretical Sorcery, was overwhelming. That, my friends, was suicide. And I knew it. I was a lord and I had a lordly manor to which I wanted to return—even if it was only to a tiny village holding to which my lovely mother and sister wished for me to return. My best choice was not girding up in steel and wading honorably into the fray. My best chance of survival was skulking in the dark and killing without mercy, an unprepared enemy.

My best chance was with the Dark Men.

CHAPTER 2
THE MISSION

At a distance, a figure slid through the brush and into view. A man in leather armor. Scimitar held before him in one hand and bone-composite bow in the other. He moved almost catlike, barely disturbing the flora around him. I sensed that he felt our presence—his head rotating slowly on his shoulders, weapons ready to strike and stepping quietly heel-toe, heel-toe. He knew an attack was forthcoming. But still, he advanced. And then, another came through the brush. And another, until four men had advanced. It seemed that was all there were, for several seconds passed and nothing else emerged from the murk.

Yet, no signal from the Darkstalker.

And then, I saw it. A presence. Barely discernible. A mere smudge in the darkness, like a reflection of Hell itself.

There was a fifth.

Nothing moved as that last figure floated along the trail—not brush, not grass, not tree limb, not even the air seemed to shift before it.

And then, the whistle came, high-pitched and shrieking.

The Dark Men fell upon them. A quick volley of crossbow bolts took the first of the bunch, and he fell like a sack of grain. Then, silently as you like, the three other Dark Men and myself, slipped silently forward to attack. Two of the heathens fell quickly. The third put up a valiant fight, but I felled him with a backhanded strike to the throat, almost severing his head completely. He slid off of my blade like a slab of pork fat and then plunked onto the earth.

The night lapsed into silence, except for the breathing of us, the four Dark Men. Where was the fifth enemy? He was good—invisible to us. Surely, Rayfe watched him from the blackness, ready to take him before he could murder us. My heart crawled into my throat and my heart raced again. Nervously, I crouched down, scanning the darkness for signs of this silent warrior, keeping my fire-blackened knife dancing back and forth in front of me. The other Dark Men did not seem to know of his presence. Fools. Could they have not seen the smudge of darkness as it trailed the enemy column?

They rifled the fallen bodies now. Not for booty or treasure—they were too disciplined for that—but for our singular mission. They searched for missives dispatched to the Il' Aruk.

I knew with certainty that, if Rayfe did not see this enemy and was not going to engage him, then I was dead. We were all dead. Where had the villain gone? Instinctively, I lowered myself. Fear slithered through me, stinging my heart into a rapid staccato. Could he see me? Could he hear my heart, beating like a mad drum?

"Aaron . . ." a growling, whispered voice in the dark. It was Theron, a sturdy killer from south of Leonay, where they bred tavern brawlers and axe-wielding Godsmen. "Can you not help us, man? Search that one near you and lets be on our—"

His sentence ended in a gurgle and I watched his burly form lurch forward to slam into the ground. One down. I hesitated, instinctively wanting to attack, but not knowing where to direct my violence. Aggressive action won battles, did it not? But move to strike what? Where there should have been an enemy, there was complete blackness.

I saw nothing. I heard nothing.

CHAPTER 3
THE BETRAYAL

"Theron?" I heard Simon call quietly, as he padded into the brush, disappearing from my sight. His call went unanswered. Simon had killed a hundred or more heathens that I myself had witnessed. He was an assassin without peer—except for Rayfe, of course—and he moved with a devil's deliberation. Yet still, I heard fear in his voice. He was gone into the darkness, tracking the ghost that had killed his friend, Theron.

But he was behaving like a damn fool. Separation meant we could be dealt with piecemeal by a wily attacker. I moved closer to Ractus, the last of us that I could yet see.

And then, Simon fell from the brush, fighting a defensive battle, parrying and blocking. "Aaron,

Ractus," Simon called out, as he flailed. "Kill the wicked bitch while I yet live." Something dark and moving fast lashed out, and Simon's parries became desperate.

I rushed forward, as did Ractus. I felt the other Dark Man moving swiftly to my left, a whirling, with the hissing of blades, as we rushed. We were quick and silent. But this murderer was quicker. With the sound of an arrow being fired through a melon, something *thunked* into Simon. I saw a flash of silver as the point of a thin blade slid out his back and quickly withdrew. A fountain of blood spewed toward me and the second Dark Man flopped to the ground.

Shite! What manner of fiend stalked us?

Then, Ractus was upon it. A step ahead of me, his black blades slicing before him, he whirled and spun, whirled and spun. His knives cut the air, missing anything solid. Still, he pressed the attack, as I barreled in from the target's flank. I could see nothing but the hint of a shape, lithe and fast. Incredibly fast. A flash of silvery metal and Ractus fell back, grasping at his throat. He gurgled, calling out in a breathy cry that died half-uttered on his lips. He slipped lifelessly to the ground.

Abandoning finesse for a fool's notion against this dexterous enemy, I lowered my head and rushed headlong, arms outstretched at where I had last seen the adversary's killing shade.

Where was Rayfe, by The God?

My body struck the enemy and I realized how light she was. I could tell it was a woman now, by the shape of her body and structure of her bones. From the power of my rush, she was lifted from the ground and thrust backward, a good ten paces. I roared along with her, pumping my legs as I ran. As we traveled through the air, I wrapped my arms about her and squeezed, my knife still gripped tightly in my fist.

I had, at the onset of this melee, considered drawing my sword. But had not, for some odd reason. I thanked The God for his small blessings. A knife was much better for this close work, I remembered thinking, as we slammed into the ground. The breath went out of her. I heard it, like a rush of air. Then wheezing. Quickly, I flipped her over and my blade flew toward her throat. She rolled away, struggling madly against my grip. Her speed was unimaginable. My knife struck the ground behind her, but I held the girl tightly. Her hand came up behind me, knife bared and metal flashing. Luckily, she was at an awkward angle and could get no strength or leverage behind the blow. Still, the blade ripped across my side and down my hip, parting the leather I wore, like paper. I felt a warm flow of blood rushing over my legs and torso. I knew if I didn't subdue her quickly, I'd surely die.

Admitting that a woman was a superior fighter would normally have been difficult for me, but right then, with my life blood spilling out, there was no denying the truth. I was clearly outmatched. She squirmed away, using her shoulder blades and hips as leverage. I was losing my grip. Grunting loudly and clenching my teeth against the pain, I went for my only advantage—raw strength. I slammed my elbow ahead and felt it crack against her face. Her nose gave way as the cartilage collapsed and she grunted aloud. Her head slammed backwards against the ground and her shimmering blade slipped from her fingers. She was dazed. I swore it to be the death of her. Spinning my knife into a slashing grip, I plunged it toward her neck.

The God knows why, but just then, I stopped. Call it conscience, foolishness or misplaced chivalry, but my heart would not let me cut this woman's head from her shoulders. I held my knife to her neck and felt the blade bite against the soft flesh there. A thin line of dark blood oozed over the blade and dripped down her painted neck. She opened her eyes and glared at me—a look of hatred, so deep and so profound, that I found my breath caught in my throat. Then, she squirmed. Not in fear, but in resistance, still trying to gain her freedom. I almost admired her for her resilience.

"Stop it, bitch!" I said, pressing the blade a little harder.

"Dog," she whispered, her voice steel. "Murdering dog!" She spat into my face. I flinched away.

The hypocrisy of the savage was almost laughable. I had seen first-hand, the handiwork of their assassins on the Faithful. Scores—hundreds—of unarmed Pilgrims butchered, like swine on the road to the Holy Land and left to rot in the sun.

I told myself to end it right then and raised the blade again. "Now, you die for butchering my friends, heathen," I said, twisting the words all I could and screwing my eyes up like a lunatic. I wanted her to be afraid. I wanted her to beg.

But her look of defiance sharpened. I'd get no request for quarter from this one.

Time to kill her.

But, something made me pause again. Was it providence or divine will that stayed my hand? Or a hearkening to a chivalric oath I once believed in? Or was it something about this particular heathen? Perhaps it was all three, in retrospect. Whatever the case, I realized suddenly that her eyes were wrong. Wrong shape—oval-like, not the almond-shaped eyes of our enemy. And wrong color. Although, in the darkness, I could not see the true color, I could tell that they were lightly tinted, perhaps green or blue or gray. Her face was charcoaled black for night fighting, so I could not verify her skin's tone, but the shape of her face was oval and narrow, not the rounded visage of the heathen. This woman—this warrior—who sliced through three of the Dark Men like freshly churned butter had come from the great Kingdom of Bannon. From home.

What kind of madness was this? Like a fool, I sat back and breathed deeply, shocked at the revelation.

That was when she struck.

CHAPTER 4
THE GHOST

The sun crept over the horizon as the fuzziness that filled my head cleared up. I lay on my back, my head throbbing and soaked with . . . sweat? No. It was blood! I tasted its coppery thickness on my lips and in my mouth. I tried to sit up, but was stopped by the point of a sword. Rayfe stood over me, his sword point at my throat—a rather obvious harbinger of a coming death.

"I should kill you myself for letting the devil-bitch get away," he said.

"Where were you?" I managed to ask, trying to keep the accusation from my voice.

He ignored my question and pressed forward with his sword. Its bite was cold and harsh. Rayfe was merciless—on his own men, as much as the enemy. Yet, I knew that the slaying would be swift—he saved the torture for the heathen. My visions of the court dissipated, and dreams of my heroic return to Greenshire melted to shite. What kind of world was it that a commoner like Rayfe could murder a knight and not be nailed to a cross? It's a testament to the demand for his skills. When a killer was as efficient and necessary as Rayfe was to a nobleman, a few knights could easily be spared to keep him satisfied. After all, it was The God's calling he was fulfilling. Weren't we all guaranteed entrance to the gates of Paradise, noble and commoner alike? I swallowed and closed my eyes, waiting for the blow. At least my exploits thus far in this Crusade had guaranteed me salvation. Hadn't they? Could one failing, such as the previous night, result in the loss of the archbishop's absolution?

The moment passed. And I yet lived.

Said Rayfe, "Unfortunately, The God has left me with the need for assistance in tracking and killing this heathen before she can reach the Il' Aruk." He continued only after a long, lingering moment. "And sadly, I find that there is no one else around but you, Aaron of Neder, to do this." He sheathed his sword and turned his back to me.

The words took a moment to register and then, washed over me like The God's Grace cleansing me of my sins. I was saved. Perhaps, by necessity only and perhaps, only for time enough for Rayfe to find another Dark Man to assist him, but for the moment, I was saved. It is these small moments for which we must be grateful. Perhaps, I chanced to hope as unlikely as it might have been, that I would see those court ladies after all.

As I stood, a rush of pain thrust through my head like a lance. Instinctively, my hand shot to my scalp, where I found a wound. Flesh parted back from the bone, running in a ragged line across my upper forehead. My fingers teased at the paper-like flesh and slid against the blood-covered skull beneath. The strangest things passed through my mind at that moment. I wondered, of course, how I'd survived such a strike. The woman's knife had obviously scored only a glancing blow. Somehow the devil had not killed me. A woman of such skill? I couldn't believe that my survival was, somehow, an accident.

I also remembered thinking that I would not be able to wear a hat anytime soon. And a helmet was out of the question. I suppressed a mad laugh and pulled my fingers away. Standing and walking would be awkward.

"You are lucky, Aaron," Rayfe said. "Her blade was not as well placed as it was with the others. You will survive, if I allow it."

"Yes . . ." was all I could think to respond. He was letting me know exactly where I stood with him. My failure was not forgotten and he would execute his threat whenever he wished. I'd known Rayfe, the Darkstalker, for some time and he was not a man that bluffed.

"You will be considerably uglier now," he added, in half-hearted jest.

But any humor that I might glean from his joking was lost in the haze of horror that had consumed my mind since I woke to his sword at my throat. My life was forfeit for my failure. It was the way of the Dark Men. Suddenly, my choice to join the Dark Men seemed foolhardy at best.

I looked toward him, doing my best to meet his cold eyes, and smiled thinly—it was all I could muster.

Some hours later we had returned to our campsite, two leagues distant from the ambush site, where the marsh was a bit flatter and the bog not so deep. There, we had left our belongings and mounts the previous night. It had taken the balance of the morning to reach the site. My legs ached and the wound on my side was tearing, sending knives of pain slicing through me, with each step. Blood still oozed in thick, red beads from the knife-wound in my skull.

"We ride from here," Rayfe said. "I have a good idea where she will emerge from this cursed swamp."

"Now?" I asked foolishly, despite knowing the answer, already. In addition to the pain, I was exhausted. If I could rest but a little longer. An hour. Two hours. Then, I would be a new man.

"War waits for no one, Aaron. Do you think the heathen is resting?" His voice was mocking, as if my need for rest was pathetic. Was it he who now bled his life onto the trail or me? But he was correct about the woman. She was moving swiftly. There was no doubt in my mind. I remembered the cold hardness in her eyes. The hate. Yes, she would not rest.

"Remember, your life depends on your actions," he added, in his matter-of-fact way.

I only nodded.

CHAPTER 5
THE INFILTRATION

I mounted old Swayback stiffly, trying to put as little pressure on my ribs as possible. I *clucked* to Swayback and turned to follow Rayfe, the Darkstalker. He rode quickly, guiding his horse through the thick brush like it was nothing. Swayback and I struggled to keep up with Rayfe and his warhorse—given to him by the duke himself. Soon, we were galloping along broken trails and barely-discernable pathways. Strangely-curved and twisted cypress trees rose like columns of infantry that had frozen in place and grown over by hanging tendrils of strangling moss. Pools of stagnant smelling water, hidden by tall grass, marched up to the sides of the trails. The blades of grass were thick and razor-like and cut at Swayback's legs and hooves, as we moved ahead. We were hot and sweaty. The leather of our clothing was soaked and creaked as we ran on.

I wasn't sure how long Swayback could keep up with Rayfe's charger. I could already feel him sweating and shuddering beneath my legs. The God save me if the old warhorse collapsed. Rayfe would be done with me, then. I spurred the old beast on. My fate, to some degree, was in the hands of the broke down animal. He would either run hard or we'd both be killed.

That thought prompted me to contemplate my situation. As I saw it, at that moment, I had two choices. Neither of which were very good. I could either redeem myself when—and if—we caught up with the heathen runner through success in battle, or I could make a run for it and get away from Rayfe. That way, Rayfe would have to choose between going after me, and accomplishing his mission.

But if I fought the woman again, I wasn't sure I could best her. In fact, the prospect was dubious at best. And if I made a dash for freedom, I'd have no chance of ever going home. The duke would find out and my family would be shamed, and stripped of their lands. And I'd be stuck in the Holy Land. Not a good solution to my way of thinking.

I'd have to kill her. That was the only solution—my only chance at survival. As fearsome as she might be, I feared the cold-hearted cruelty and wicked efficiency of Rayfe, more so. I'd face her and I'd kill her. Or I would die in the trying.

We rode in strange silence as allies of necessity who held little love or respect for one another. He said nothing to me and I had no desire to utter a word to him. The leagues faded behind us in steady measures, the trees turning to stunted oak and birch and sycamore. The ground hardened to soft muck, leaving the bog behind. Another half-day and we would be on the flats. And then, it was a sprint. The woman had no horse, so the advantage was passing to us. But if she were able to evade them for a full day, she'd reach Gorak, the outer limits of Gol Toran.

If she reached the walls of Al' Torak, the race was lost.

Our pace increased. I felt Rayfe's intensity, his excitement at the prospect of catching the woman, as the woods fell away. The energy was catchy. Even Swayback was running steadily, his breathing constant and measured. Still, the Darkstalker put distance between us, as his charger found its head in the opening landscape. I resisted the urge to push my mount any harder. If I went much faster or much longer, he'd die, to be sure.

Night approached and already, the grayness of dusk made it difficult to see my companion. He was far out ahead now, riding as though the Devil himself was on our trails. It was not so far from the truth, though perhaps reversed. We were chasing the offspring of the Devil to my way of thinking.

As darkness came fully upon us, I reigned in my charger and peered around. Rayfe was nowhere to be seen.

"Shite!" I cursed out loud. I'd pay for this for sure. I spurred the beast harder now, driving ahead near panic.

I rode blindly for less than a span, my heart thudding against my ribs, as I considered the implications of my losing the Darkstalker. Then, I heard a voice come out of the darkness. Shortly, a figure loomed out of the black and I yanked hard on Swayback's reigns.

"Bring him to heal, knight. We stop here for the night."

Rayfe. The man was a cursed ghost. We skidded to a halt and I vaulted from my saddle to stand before him, my breathing ragged and my heart teetering on madness. Thank The God I'd found him. My Redemption at the Gates of Heaven was just delayed again. I let out a long, labored breath. "Rayfe," I said. "I thought I'd lost you."

"You did," he said, grimly. "Best be rid of that worn out nag," he added in that gravelly voice of his, waiving a hand at my loyal horse.

"He's been in the family for—"

"I don't care. He'll get you killed one day. Can't run. Can't hear. He's a danger to you, knight."

I chose not to respond. I wondered if he knew how poor my family was. That this warhorse, the armor and sword that had accompanied me, was all the family could afford—the lion's share of our wealth. Neder was not a wealthy lordship. We raised only a hundred acres of grain. Most was taxed by the duke annually and the rest . . . well, the rest barely fed the peasants that farmed it for us. It was another reason that I had undertaken the Crusade. Perhaps, I could gain favor or treasure in my travels. Another load of shite. Most died in this hole of piss. Those that didn't die, returned back wealthy in stories of courage and Honor and battle, but little else.

"We rest here, eh?" I asked. After riding so hard, it seemed strange to me that we would rest now. But, I wasn't about to complain. The prospect of a good nap was a gift from The God. Reaching up to my bedroll, I began unstrapping my kit from the rump of my steed.

"We rest here," the Darkstalker confirmed. "But you won't need that. We won't be staying that long. A span. No more." He waived at my head and then, to my side. "Enough to get our wind," he finished.

He actually seemed to care about my wellbeing. It was not like him at all and I felt suspicious hackles rise on my neck.

"We must be ready to ride," he said. "Lest the heathen you let escape reaches the Il' Aruk. As it is, we're likely ahead of her, thanks to the route that we took and the speed of our mounts."

"Of course," I said. "Ready to ride." I led Swayback to a nearby elm, dropped the reigns and slid against the trunk. In mere moments, I was asleep.

Chapter 6

The Interrupted Escape

I awoke, lying on my side. My wrists were bound and my knives and sword thrown clear of any hope of reaching them. The sun was just above the horizon and the day's heat was already starting to seep into the early morning cool. My heart crawled into my throat as I considered what the situation meant for me. I looked about, desperately. Any thought of Redemption, of finding the heathen and killing her, was lost in the feeling of helplessness that now descended on me. She must have come upon us, as we slept. But hadn't Rayfe been on watch? I'd assumed as much when I'd fallen asleep.

I struggled against the bonds and squirmed on the ground, trying to find a way to free myself. But it was no use. The ropes were too tight. Still, I had another dirk in my boot. I could feel it pressing against my ankle. Thank The God they hadn't searched me well enough to find it. I still had a chance, however slim it might be.

"He wakes," a voice said. A woman's voice. I knew when I heard, it that I was on my way to Heaven's gates. I'd find out soon enough about my promised Absolution.

A face pressed against mine, a knee crushed down on my hands, secured behind my back. "Good morning, beautiful." Rayfe's voice curdled through me in warm breath that smelled of shite.

"You?" I asked. I was incredulous. Words failed me. The idea that Rayfe was in on this treason—and not dead—was not one that I would have ever considered. Like I said earlier, he was the best of us.

"Me," he said, back. "Yes, me."

He ran a hard finger along the cut in my head. Pain sizzled along my face and down my neck. I pulled away.

He continued, "You should have surmised that I was involved. Why else would I have left you alone during the ambush? Have you ever known me to not take part in killing?" He asked the question that had lingered on my mind last night. "You have never been the wisest of the Dark Men." He smiled crookedly, like the Devil about to harvest the soul of a fool he'd already tainted beyond Redemption.

His insult was lost on me. I had already accused myself of such stupidity—and much worse.

"You are a traitor." I stated the obvious. I spat into his face—a time tested tradition of defiance. There was nothing left of which to be afraid. I was already dead.

He struck me, then. Hard. Across the cheek. The sting of his studded glove slammed across my face, taking skin, crushing the soft bones of my nose and re-opening the gash on my head. It sent me sprawling back to the ground beneath, where I rolled over and groaned. When I recovered enough to sit back up, I looked him in the eye, trying to maintain some dignity. Some Honor.

"Aren't we all?" he asked.

"Darkstalker, enough!" the woman's voice demanded.

Rayfe huffed and stood. "If not for your gold, whore, I'd kill him, sure. And then, have some fun with you."

"Perhaps," she said. But there was no fear in her voice.

She'd drawn her curved, short sword again and paced warily behind him. I could see her now, better than the night past. Her face was painted black and dark green. Long, yellow hair was weaved in a tight tail that hung down her back. And the curves of a woman's body could not be hidden beneath the dull, leather jerkin she wore over a heavy, green shirt. She wore leather gloves and high, black boots. A dirk was strapped to her right boot. A saber hung from her hip, and the empty scabbard for her short sword.

"One day, we may find out, murderer," said she, to Rayfe. "Now step away from him. I must speak to the assassin. As it is, I need him, and you have taken my gold. Or don't you remember?"

He nodded and stepped away, striding to his horse to dig through his kit.

She took his place over me, crouched low, so her face was an arm's length distance from mine. "You have murdered the helpless," she hissed at me, pressing the point of her dirk into my cheek. I pulled away and she giggled madly. "Yet, still I find myself in need of you. I'd rather kill you now."

I wanted to lash out. I wanted to say that she had killed innocents, too. That her self-righteous heathen allies had killed more than their share. But the comment was hollow. Yes, they had. And yes, we had. Did that excuse my murder?

But, Rayfe. Who was he? How had this happened? He had murdered more than me, more than all of us. He was the Darkstalker—the most hated man in Gol Toran. If she was so damn righteous, how had she struck a deal with the likes of him?

"What of him?" I asked and nodded my head toward Rayfe. He crouched some distance away now, his back to us, fingers drifting over the ornate workings on a silver-laden coffer. Gold and gems inside glittered up at him.

"He is the worst of you," she said. "He kills for no reason, other than the pleasure of killing. But he was a simple matter of gold and promises of treasure. He cares not who he butchers."

"And why? How would you trust him? He sold out his own. He murdered hundreds of the heathen. Why would you recruit him?"

"There is a bigger vision, fool. The end of this war. An end that means that the Crusaders will not return. That is the endgame here. And because we offer him more gold than your duke could offer, that is how I trust him. Is it not ironic that we can turn the most dedicated of the archbishop's murderers with little more than coin? And more, the Il' Aruk cares nothing of nobility or blood rites. When this war is over and he rules all of Gol Toran, including your Holy Land and your Holy City, he can be whatever he wants and do whatever he wants. He needs no title or blood-endowed privileges to be a lord. His exploits here guarantee him wealth and prestige beyond anything your archbishop or your duke can offer." She spat on the ground. Her eyes turned cold. A weakness in this alliance perhaps? She obviously hated the idea of working with the man.

"What of his Redemption? What of his rights to enter Paradise? How can you offer him this?"

She spat again. "There is no such thing. The Kingdom of Heaven and your archbishop's damnable Three Covenants. They are all lies. Haven't you realized that? It is a tool. A tool to make foolish men, such as you, sacrifice yourselves to enrich him and the Grand Temple of The Star."

"Sacrilege," I said, with as much indignity as I could find. "You shall find out when The God calls us home. You shall realize the madness of your choices." But there was no heart in my response. I wasn't sure if I believed it myself. I added, "What of your Il' Aruk? Does he not promise the same as the archbishop?"

"He is as foolish as the archbishop. Let me show you . . ."

She unstrung her leather top and pulled down her collar, revealing the firm, rounded shape of her breast. I tried to look away from the woman, long-forgotten Chivalric oaths bubbling up in me. I was uncomfortable, even as I faced death, to look openly upon the beauty of womanly flesh. She laughed aloud. "Your modesty reflects well on you," she uttered. She pulled my chin around so that I could not avoid staring at her exposed breast. "Look," she said. Branded there, around the tip of the breast, in light blue and white ink, was the Five Pointed Star of The God.

I gasped aloud. She was a Vestal—one of the Wives of The God. "God," I hissed. "What have you done?"

"I know The God's mind," she whispered. "I have served him closer than most. I know His heart and that of his archbishop. And they are cold and hard!" Her eyes drifted off to some-place else and she lapsed into a monotone voice. I went silent, listening intently to the once-Vestal. "I was taken by the Il' Aruk," she said, at length, "in a raid on a train of Pilgrims."

"Then, you know," I said, meeting her eyes. "You know the savagery of the heathen. How . . . why . . . have you forsaken . . . ?"

"Me? Forsaken Him? It is He that abandoned me, fool. I committed myself to His mercy, and he left me there on that dirty road to hell, savaged by heathens and taken by their king."

But why had she cloven to the Il' Aruk, instead of resisting, if she thought as little of him as her own God? If they had raped her and killed her party? I left the question unasked, however. There were other, more pressing questions to get answered. "What are your plans for me?" I asked. "What do you two traitors have in mind for me?"

Rayfe's voice ground into me from behind. "We need you. You, dear Aaron, are critical to our plans."

"What? How can I be critical to your plans? I am naught, but a hedge knight from a lowly house. I'm nothing to the duke."

"No. Don't be a buffoon," she said, leaning in close. Her breath was warm on my face. I tried to turn away, but she held my jaw firmly in her hand. She spoke again. "You are a Dark Man. Your word is golden. What's more, you were sent with the Darkstalker to kill the missive, to stop word of the siege from reaching the Il' Aruk."

"Huh? I don't understand," I said. And I didn't. What could they possibly have in mind for me?

"You shall take word to the duke," Rayfe said.

"Word of what?"

"Why, word of my death," he responded, with a strange twinkle in his eye. "And the death of this lovely, missive-carrying bitch." Rayfe's hands slipped through her hair and pulled her up to him. He leaned in and let his lips slide over her painted cheek. His tongue lashed out and slashed across her lips and throat.

She slid her knife up to his throat, then yanked away from him and cast him an angry scowl. "Yes, you shall tell him that no message has made it through," she said, never taking her eyes off her ally. "That you killed the runner. And that you are the only survivor."

"And if I don't?"

"Simple, my lord." Rayfe twisted the words to emphasize exactly how much it meant to be a minor knight in this crusade. "If you don't, I'll kill you. But first, I shall return to our home and butcher your whole family. Slowly, I might add."

Chapter 7
The Ambush

It seemed I had little choice but to conspire with the traitors. The decision should have been an easy one. I was, after all, a mercenary of sorts. My survival being all that was important in the end—or so it was that drove my Crusade thus far. But something deep inside, buckled and railed against this task. Honor? Duty? Whatever it was, it was buried under years of neglect.

Was there something stronger than one's desire to survive? The protection of one's family? Perhaps the decision would have been easier if the threat against my sister and parents didn't hang in my mind's eye, like an ominous black cloud. I could see them in our manor's grand hall, hanging by their ankles from the thick, oak rafters, their throats slit so deep that puddles of blackish blood formed pools deep enough to drown in.

I considered whether Rayfe would make good on such a threat and trek all the way to Neder in the Duchy of Greenshire, just to exact a measure of vengeance. But from a year or more of campaigning with him, I knew Rayfe's black heart, as well as anyone. He'd travel across the world to maintain his reputation, to exact revenge on a man who'd crossed him.

I'd once seen him infiltrate the keep at Gol Taran—indeed, I'd taken part in the task—and gut the handmaidens of an Earless who'd dared demand that he leave the court of her husband because of his low birth. On his way out, he'd left a ragged scar on the face of the Earless' young son. That day, she'd learnt the standing of a warrior, like Rayfe, in a world shaped by warfare. Even her husband, a powerful lord in the Holy Land and prominent in the Crusade—if not back in Bannon—had not dared send men to avenge his son's disfigurement. Such was the mystique of the Darkstalker. She'd not questioned his heritage again and I'd not questioned his capacity for murder and vengeance. Ever. His soul was as dark as the Devil's Pit. Yes. He'd make the trip. And yes, he'd murder my family and hang them from the beams.

She leaned over and cut the leather straps securing my wrists. Rayfe stood behind her with my weapons, gathered up and wrapped about with my sword's belt. I briefly considered making a play for my boot knife, but dismissed that as stupidity. I might be able to get one of them by surprise, but they were both more superior in weapons mastery, than I. If I were to attempt such a stunt, I was sure that they'd kill me. My best chance of survival was doing as I was told.

I kept my gaze level, locked on her eyes. Like facing down a dog, showing fear ensured eventual death. But as our eyes met, I saw something there, behind the hate and rage that smoldered on the surface. Was it sadness? Compassion?

Or my imagination?

Did it matter? It was gone before I knew it. Women, like men, do things in war that they normally wouldn't do. They do them even when they know the actions are wrong. I'd done it a hundred times. And she was about to do it, too. I felt it. I saw it in those ice-blue eyes.

When I had freed my hands and rubbed the circulation back into them, Rayfe handed me my sword and knives. "Ride south, to the duke's bivouac. We were to meet him tomorrow by mid of night."

"Where do you go?" I asked.

"We go to the Fort at Al' Torak, to see the Il' Aruk," she responded. "Your captain goes with me as evidence that our ploy has been success-ful." She handed me a satchel—her missive bag. "You took this from my corpse, Dark Man," she said, in a traitorous tone. "Take it to your duke."

She smiled at me. It wasn't dark or evil or cold. It was sad. She knew what this had cost me. She knew that, what I went to do, was beyond any-thing that I could have ever imagined. It was a betrayal not only of myself, but of The God and an entire race of people. It was nothing less than the loss of promised Absolution for the price of my family.

"Do not follow us, Aaron," Rayfe offered up, without any prodding. "You are no match for me. And the Vestal will lay wards on our camp. You will be detected, if you try. And you and your family will be forfeit for your foolishness."

Strangely, I had not considered killing them in their sleep or taking them from the shadows. Now, the idea rushed through my mind, fresh and excited. And the thought was powered by a new revelation. He would not have mentioned such a thing if he was not afraid of me following. He was worried about me. The strange feeling of elation that surged in my heart, surprised me. Was I so concerned for his approval? Or did I have such a need to prove myself? Being a threat to Rayfe was the best a warrior could ask for.

He was right, of course. They were both better fighters than me. But I knew Rayfe. I knew his methods and tactics. I knew his strengths and failings. Perhaps, there was still a chance.

But could this woman really cast Wards? I had seen the heathen's Sorcerers flinging fire and lightning into formations of Crusaders and freezing ranks of infantry where they marched. But could she be a Sorcerer? Is this how she moved without being seen? Killed without noise? It was an unforgivable sacrilege, for which burning was the only punishment. For a Vestal to trade in the dark arts was . . . well, it was something that I did not understand and something which terrified me.

"I will ride to the duke and tell him of your demise, Rayfe," I said, even as I contemplated my next course of action. They both nodded in that way that soldiers do to each other. That way of saying, '*good luck, wind at your back*' and all that. It was noncommittal and I was grateful for it.

I collected my weapons from Rayfe, mounted up, bid them farewell and then, rode out of there as fast as Swayback would carry me.

My charger ate up the ground. For a span, the land fell away behind me. Soon, I rode into a draw between two rising spurs. The trees grew thicker there. Elms and mulberries. I pulled up my steed and dismounted. It was hard to think in the saddle. I opened the case she'd given me and pulled out the missive—the lie, as I had begun to think of it. The parchment rested in my hand, as heavy as lead.

Al' Torak was two days' ride distant, to the west. The duke's bivouac was a similar distance to the South and East, along the Pilgrim's Approach. The choices were as divergent in their meaning as they were in their direction. One choice took me toward Honor and almost certain death. The other guaranteed me dishonor—at least in the traditional sense—but, likely survival. My choice would have been easy two days earlier.

Go to where you will survive. Go to the duke. Tell the lie.

But something in the woman's look had told me otherwise. She knew what she was asking. Even hoped I'd do it. But, the lie meant the destruction of the duke and his army—thousands of Crusaders. I told myself that thousands would die anyway. That it was meaningless. One more massacre in a never-ending stream of massacres. And perhaps, she was right, that total destruction of this Crusade would end the foolhardy invasions from my homeland and those that worshiped The God. Perhaps the destruction of the duke and his men would mean the end to all of the madness. Forever, just like she said.

But, forever is a long time and the rightness of the cause suddenly didn't matter. Whether the Il' Aruk or the archbishop or the duke emerged from this struggle as the ruler of the Holy City was not my concern. Those questions were for bigger men than I. Those questions were for The God to answer.

What was suddenly clear to me was that I would be judged on my actions. Whether by The God or me, by my family or my enemies. In my heart, I realized with an unexpected clarity now, that it was my actions that determined my Honor.

And I had to live with them for the rest of my days.

CHAPTER 8
THE
NECROMANCER

If I rode hard, I could catch them. They'd likely stay to the main roads. If they did, they would reach Al' Torak by nightfall, tomorrow. I wanted to catch them by nightfall, tonight. Coming upon them during the day would take away any semblance of surprise that I might glean from such an act.

I smelled rain in the wind. It would be the first of spring, if it came. Back home, it would signal the Spring's Celebration—the renewal of life. I smiled for a moment at the memories of my sister and I, six summers old, hand in hand and moving to the circle-dance—our traditional dance that welcomed life from The God. I missed home now, more than I should have. The fear that was ever-present had buried the fact that I missed my family. Suddenly, it had surfaced painfully, and I wanted much to return.

I swallowed it back. Such childish sentiments would only serve to get me killed. Lowering my head, I spurred old Swayback on.

Rain began to fall as the darkness of night consumed me. First it came in small, misting drizzle. And then, larger drops hammered into the ground, in tiny spouts. Within the hour, it came in roaring sheets. It was still hot. It was hot all the time in this damn place. Water slid across my filthy face, feeling more like warm, sticky shit, than a refreshing spring shower. I wiped my hand across my face and whipped the slushy muck onto the ground, letting the cleansing water take its place. I looked upward and into the downfall, letting it spread over my cheeks, before pulling my hood over my head. Enough stalling, I thought, and I wheeled Swayback and headed west toward the Il' Aruk—and certain death.

I started out at a fast lope, but was soon forced to slow my ride. The rain had already turned the earth to muck. It was too dangerous to ride so quickly in the dark of night with such poor footing. But I was grateful for the noise. My quarry had likely stopped and pitched camp. They had no reason to hurry. I hoped that I had guessed right. If I had, I would be upon their camp, shortly. Another span and I dismounted.

There was a bridge just ahead . . . I walked Swayback to the bank and tethered him to a storm-shattered oak covered in hanging moss. I remembered from previous campaigns that the river was only chest deep. I waded into the rushing current.

I was correct about the depth, although the rain had already raised the river. It slid past my neck at its deepest point. I slugged past a momentary fear that I would wash away, pushed the dread back, and cordoned it off in the back of my mind. If I thought too much about the many fears that haunted me right then, I'd have fled back into the night.

After some time, the water receded. I climbed the far bank. Through the trees, I could make out the flickering orange glow of a distant campfire.

It had to be them.

As quietly as I could, I drifted through the twisted oaks and elms. I kept to where the brush was thickest and the grass the highest—and always guided by that orange light. I crept like the dead, moving as slowly as time would allow. All my years of training and experience came down to these few moments. My family's lives depended on it. My army depended on it. It was a daunting feeling, but I was rewarded in my patience. Luck favored me, and I made no mistakes, as the grass crushed silently beneath my boots. No vines caught on my jerkin. No jingling of sword in the scabbard. No unwanted sneezes visiting me when I least wanted it. I had never felt such exhilaration.

Still, the rain fell.

Finally, I reached the outskirts of the camp. My visibility was severely limited by the darkness and the rain, so I padded silently up to the edge of the trees, as close as I could get, without alerting the inhabitants. Beyond, their horses were tethered to a rope slung between two trees. A fire still burned in the center of camp, tended by a man with his back to me. I reckoned it was Rayfe. The woman was a lump, snoozing comfortably between me and the fire. Neither had pitched a tent against the rain. Except for their leathers and weapons, which they wore, their equipment lay in a pile near the horses, inundated.

I knew that if I failed, my family would die. It was a risk that meant everything to me. And a risk that meant nothing to the outcome of the coming fight. But if I had a choice, I'd kill Rayfe first. I doubted much that the Vestal would follow a vengeance pact for a man she likely hated more than I did.

So, then. Rayfe first and then, the Vestal.

The Darkstalker was distant at twenty paces. My plan was to creep the first ten and then, it would be a quick, deadly sprint to take him by surprise. I drew my sword and silently advanced into the campsite.

"I smell you, Aaron," his voice came out of the darkness. "Your stink even comes to me through this damnable rain."

I froze. Wavered.

". . . and hear you," he added. "You have done the most foolish thing this night."

"I did the only thing, I could," I answered, trying to keep my voice steady. Hoping to catch him unaware, I rushed while he still sat by the fire. But he had been prepared for it and, whirling around, he produced a knife from somewhere in his jacket, batted aside my blade and slid it up across my jerkin, tearing a hole through the protective leather. But the armor saved me and his knife didn't find purchase in my flesh. I stepped back, shocked at the speed of his movement, and held my sword up before me. He smiled widely, like a hungry wolf.

"It's time to die, Aaron," he said.

He pressed the attack, a whirlwind of steel and blades. I could not hope to keep parrying his blows. My sword was heavier and more deadly than his knives. But he was fast, almost a blur to me. I backed towards the woods and he moved more quickly, dancing through the camp-site. He came in low and I parried. Then high, and I ducked. He spun sideways and around and I lunged with my blade, cutting only air, as his dagger's blade slipped down my left arm, open-ing me to the bone. I howled and stumbled back-ward.

Sensing victory—and rightfully so—he came on more quickly.

That is when something happened that I could not have expected. Rayfe misplaced his forward foot and slipped on the wet grass. He went to a knee, his forward momentum taking him head-long past me, grasping for any hand hold. I saw his other knee twist sideways, at right angles to its natural setting, and he called out in agony. He crashed into the mud and rolled up next to the Vestal who, even now, was leaping to her feet and drawing her weapons.

I'd spent my Crusader life taking advantage of opportunities as they presented themselves to me. This moment was no different. With no hes-itation at all, I rushed forward and thrust down-ward with my sword. As I came on, the woman stumbled backward and Rayfe struggled to his one, good knee. But he was too hurt to move quickly, and the point of my long sword thrust into his chest. And just like that, Rayfe, the greatest assassin of the Third Crusade, expired on the end of my sword.

Behind him, the Vestal mumbled in a strange language I'd never heard. I rotated half a turn to face her, just as an unnatural darkness inundated the campsite. I rushed her last location and swung my weapon in a wide arch, hoping to catch anyone before me, but unable to see more than a few inches. Again, luck was with me, and my blade bit into flesh. As it did, the unnatural veil of black dissipated, leaving us, thank The God, in the night's darkness.

My sword tore across her abdomen and up her ribs. It would have been a killing blow if she wasn't so agile. As it was, it did not penetrate the rib cage and inflict mortal damage. But still, I felt ribs yield and snap beneath my blade and the flesh gave way, like churned cream. She staggered under its impact. I pressed the attack, thinking myself at an advantage, and surged ahead with another thrust.

It was a fool's move.

I saw the attack coming. I had over-extended my strike and put too much momentum into the attack. My sword missed her clean, as she dodged sideways, and her sword descended toward me. The blade tore down my leg, splitting open my thigh. I screamed into the night as I stumbled past her and pounded into a nearby tree. She staggered toward me as I turned, her own wounds slowing her considerably. Then, some kind of seizure or pain hit her, and she trembled mightily. She dropped her curved blade to the ground and staggered against another tree.

In an instant, she recovered and pulled herself up, tall. Despite the wound, my sword had torn in her side. As she faced me, concentration etched across the pain on her face. She favored her unwounded side, and her hands rose, working whatever sorcery she was about to release on me. Tendrils of darkness began to dance through the night, toward me. Realizing that my life was soon to be consumed, I lunged forward as quickly as I could. The pain in my ruined leg blazed up my back and the re-opened wound on my side tore deeper into me.

I crashed into her again, taking her full in the side, before she could finish her curse. We fell to the ground, gasping. I felt her leg snap beneath me, crunching like the worn axle on an old wagon. She cried out and then, the wind was blown from her lungs, as I slammed down on top of her. She lay there, twisted up and broken, gasping for air, like a dying fish. Blood poured out of the wound in her side and bubbled up pink and foamy at her lips.

I gathered myself up and pressed my knife to her throat. I'd been here before. She was healthy and alive. Now, I hesitated . . . again. I hadn't noticed before how beautiful she was and it slowed my hand. I just couldn't kill her. She regained her breath and calmed herself. But I could see in her eyes that she was finished. Dull and blue. No life left within.

"You spared me once, Dark Man," she whispered, and I felt a warmth flow into her. I expected hate and rage. It was disconcerting. "Now, I ask that you spare me, again."

I looked down at her quizzically. My hand was shaking and my heart racing. Sheets of rain poured over me, thudding against my leather jerkin and rolling over my back in broad waterfalls. Her eyes drilled into mine—blue and warm and forgiving. I knew then, what she wanted. Tears welled up inside me, only to be lost in the rain and sweat.

"Send me home," she hissed out between coughs, as she labored to breathe through her cracked ribs and squirming against the pain in her wounded legs.

"Yes, lady," I choked out.

She smiled at me, her lips thin and quivering with exertion. Then, she mouthed a 'thank you' as I slipped my knife between her ribs. With a last breathy gasp, her eyes rolled up into her head and the life went out of her.

I never knew her name.

CHAPTER 9
THE DECISION

Two months later, I clambered down the gangplank of the old cog onto the docks at Greenshire. Unlike the sticky heat of the Holy Land, it was cold in the Kingdom of Bannon and it made my bones creak and my back shiver. The river Weld flowed steadily underneath, rocking the vessel slightly at its moorings. I peered for a moment over my shoulder from where I had come.

The ocean and Clurak were far behind. The trip back had been excruciating—filled with the rocking, creaking ship and sick passengers, exotic animals brought back from the Crusade and terrible, half-rotten rations. We had marched to the Crusade in long columns of infantry and cavalry.

I had saved the Crusade from certain destruction. The Holy City had fallen and the duke remained in the Holy Land. Most of his knights and retainers remained behind with him. He awaited his coronation as the King of The Holy Star, the Holy defender, by the archbishop. It would be difficult, if not impossible, for the Il' Aruk to dislodge him from the high stone walls of Clurak, now.

For that, I had been honored by the duke and bestowed a Thaynehold in the eastern reaches of Greenshire—granted it was one previously held by a childless man who'd been slain in this bloody endeavor).

Yet, I returned home alone, on a sad, inglorious wooden ship.

The Vestal's eyes still visited me at night. Sometimes cold and hard and full of rage, and sometimes warm and grateful. I woke regularly, looking for her knife to be slipping across my throat. But she never came. Still, she was there, always. A vision of The God that had turned on me, the Crusade that had promised Absolution at the price of my Honor . . . and much more.

I staggered the last few feet of the plank toward my sister, arms outstretched to receive her. Just as I reached her, a lancing pain raced up my spine. I staggered and nearly fell. The wound that the Vestal had given me nagged constantly—a reminder of my murderous deeds.

My sister caught me in her arms, enveloping me and holding me upright. It was warm, comfortable there, like when we were children.

"Welcome home," she whispered.

BLUE EYES AT NIGHT

NIGHT

JP WILDER

EDGE WEAVER LLC

CONTENTS

CHAPTER 1
THE HAUNTING

R ivershire Abbey's bells echoed in the distance, calling home the saints and the approach of the Devil's hour. I stumbled and nearly fell, so deep was I in my cups. But my companion, slight thing that she was, bore my weight like a soldier.

"My lord, Aaron, perhaps we should retire," she said and giggled, her voice barely audible above the bells and the debilitating effect of too much wine.

Unable to find any sort of stability in the constantly shifting room, I leaned heavily upon the girl and grasped with my other hand the corner of a heavy table. We stood inside Rivershire Keep's great room where we feasted during festivals and events of significance. It was dark this night, lit only by two lanterns mounted on the opposite wall. Everything was shrouded in the haziness of too much libation.

What I could discern was the disapproving gaze on my sister's face. It was always there when I acted the fool. She was too honest to disguise it. I cast down my eyes, unwilling to meet the condemnation there. Had she a right? She had not seen what I had in the last Crusade, done what I had done. A fool's question. She not only had the right. She had the responsibility.

She had become my conscience.

She stood beyond the long table, near a black hole that must have been an open door. I knew, however consumed with drink I was, that she would not cast me out, nor would she chastise me, or my companion. My sister was too forgiving for such behavior.

My guilt was its own punishment.

I pulled my companion closer, thankful for her acceptance and her willingness. What was her name? I suppose it did not matter. I did not need a name for her to serve her purpose, to vanquish dark memories, if only for a brief while.

Pushing my guilt down into wine-induced oblivion, I swept my hand wide and pointed toward the portal that led to my apartments. "Lead on," I slurred and gripped her playfully.

I stumbled forward. The girl stumbled with me.

I awoke in my bed in the small hours of the morning, sweating so profusely the linens clung to my skin, and the feathered mattress was hardened by my own perspiration. It was early autumn and the tenth night in a long, dark cycle of bad nights—the longest uninterrupted series I could remember. Beside me, the young woman breathed heavily and contentedly. So deep was I in my cups the past night that I had forgotten her name. By The God, I'd forgotten she was even there.

A fire raged in the hearth like some demon bent on devouring me. I could not bear another such night.

"Shite, it's hot," I cursed. By The God, warm is good, but hot enough to cook flesh is not. I threw off the woolen blanket and lay, naked as the day I was born, staring at the shadowy ceiling. But the heat was not what had awakened me. Again the damn dream tormented me—a specter sent from Gol Toran. The Crusade, it seemed, would not leave me. What I'd done would forever be my burden. This was not an outcome which registered happily. I was young and spending the remaining years of my life fearing the coming of sleep, or worrying that some ghost lurked behind every darkened doorway, intent on driving me to madness, was no kind of existence. There are better ways to live.

There are better ways to die.

The dream was always very real—as though I were there, flesh and blood. Truth be told, it was not a dream at all. It was a memory, a vile experience that had plagued me since the fateful day outside Clurak a year or more past. And as clear as though it were yesterday.

On that terrible day, I had slain the traitor, Rayfe the Darkstalker. But that was not the source of my troubles. The same night, I had slipped a knife between the ribs of an apostate Nun who'd turned coat and become an assassin of Al' Aruk. Ostensibly, I had perpetrated the act to save the Duke's siege of the Holy City. But there was a voice deeper inside me that whispered otherwise.

It said I had killed a reflection of myself.

Once I had foolishly believed that having the Archbishop's Absolution would free me from my worldly demons. But there I lay, unable to find peace, plagued with visions of a heathen apostate whom I had murdered. An act that was the most noble and the most ghastly thing I had ever done.

That said much, because I had committed many ghastly acts.

"Send me home," she'd begged as I'd sliced her open.

Since that day, the apostate's eyes had followed me everywhere, dull and blue and empty. They watched me from the blackness behind open windows or the shadowed recesses of my keep's corridors. At night, the Vestal came to me as if girded for murder, painted black and dressed in her leathers. Often I saw the star-shaped tattoo of The God circling her disembodied breast, hovering in the darkness. When my life seemed especially comfortable or happy, her icy eyes, filled with coldness and hate, visited me as they had been before I'd snuffed their light. But more often, I saw her beautiful, terrible face gazing up at me, broken and wounded, coughing those fateful words through bloodied lips. "Send me home."

A knock at the door drew me from my thoughts. In no condition to entertain, I did not wish to be bothered so I ignored it at first. But, the knock came again.

I rose from my bed and, nursing a stabbing pain in my head, opened the door. Ser Willem, captain of the keep's guard stood outside, his armor and surcoat immaculate, young face grim and hard. His sand-colored hair was short and well groomed. He rested his left hand comfortably upon the pommel of his long sword, his other gripping the buckle on his sword belt.

He bent to me, slightly at the waist. "My lord."

"Willem," I said and my head throbbed with the effort. I waived away the formality.

I noticed Abbot Pryor stood behind him in the shadows, candle clutched in his hand. His black hair was pulled back tight, beard close cropped, dark eyes narrowed. He wore his red Abbot's robe, the golden Star of The God embroidered on his breast, glittering in the candlelight.

"My lord," said Abbot Pryor.

I leaned against the doorframe and nodded. "Father. What brings you two here so early?"

"I wish I could say it was happy news, my lord," Pryor said. He shouldered past Ser Willem and handed me a rolled piece of parchment, which I took with much hesitation. The scroll was heavy in my hands, its surface gritty and rough. I rolled it over my fingers, its meaning filled with both threat and promise. My fingers found the red wax seal, the five-pointed Star encircled with tear drops: the Archbishop's seal. I breathed deeply and pried it open.

I didn't need to. I knew what lay within.

"The Archbishop is preaching a Crusade," Pryor said, his voice a gravelly whisper, his mouth twisted into a toothy grin.

Weeks earlier the call for a new Crusade had sounded across Rivershire. It started with a missive from the Temple of The Star, beseeching me—and other nobles, of course—to ride in defense of The God. The call was full of the same promises of Absolution and Glory that had first lured me into the Holy Land—lands held by the heathen Gols. Soon after, the criers in Rivershire's streets hocked the Three Covenants: Honor, Conversion, and Redemption.

Their song beckoned me once more. And I was hard-pressed to resist.

I nodded to the Abbot and dismissed the two with a wave of my hand. After closing the door, I went to my writing table, lit a candle, and opened the document.

Thayne Aaron of Rivershire, Savior of Clurak--

The Gols have reformed under a fearsome general known as the Ek Inir Ahn. He is a savage incarnation of the Devil. His armies of murderers and Sorcerers are driving our lords from the ring of frontier forts known as the Knuckles, forts that have stood as solid, undefeated sentinels against the Gols and their heathen allies for a hundred years. Now, the Knuckles threaten to fall under a mass of Godless savages. You of all believers, know what is at stake.

As you know, your once-liege, the Duke of Greenshire, with whom you rode on the last great Crusade, brother to the King of Bannon, will be named as King of Clurak, the Holy Defender. The Devil is raising the Pit itself to stop it.

The God beseeches you, among all be-

lievers, to take up the Star and strike down these heathens and free the Holy Land from their shadow of the Gols. Go with all possible haste!

—Yours, in the Light of The God.

I tossed it upon my reading table. The document filled me with both a deep sadness for the blood that would be spilled in this Crusade and a fierce, almost hunger-like longing for days spent in the saddle, running the heathen to ground. Those days when I knew my singular purpose, no matter how grim, when the threat of death was ever-present and living to see another sunset was gift enough forever.

I stood from the table and found my way to the window. I rubbed my palm across my forehead and flicked away a layer of sweat. I threw open the sash, pushing the shutter wide. Outside, the rain pelted across the land, and a gust of wind forced a surge of cool wetness against me.

"Shite," I exclaimed. The cold, wet wind was a surprise after the warmth of my bed, and a shudder ran the length of my spine. Outside I spied the figure of a raven on the far battlement. It sat in the rain, seeking no shelter, its gaze fixed toward my window. The creature's eyes seemed to burn icy-blue and held me motionless. Then, it was gone. I remember thinking it was a waking dream or some continuation of my night terrors. I shook the vision away and rubbed sleep from my eyes.

The woman in my bed stirred.

How far had I fallen from my vows of honor and chastity, that I'd treat a woman as such? How far had I devolved that my momentary plea-sure—momentary forgetfulness of the deeds that I had done—would drive me to such acts of depravity, to sully her thusly? Once, I was a knight by virtue and deed. No longer. I'd proven that I could hide from my memories within the softness of a woman's embrace or the bottom of a flagon of ale. I could not live with this version of myself for long.

The last thing I wanted was to speak to her. I'd have to reveal I'd forgotten her name. It was not the first time I'd avoided such unpleasantries by asking the castle servants to escort a lady quietly from the keep. But alas, it was not to be.

"Come to bed, Lord Aaron," she whispered, low and sultry. Sleep still clung to her voice.

The idea was not without merit, but the reprieve would be fleeting. The memories always found me.

"Not now ... um ... my lady. Return to sleep," I said, but needn't have, for the sound of her heavy breathing indicated she'd already drifted.

I sat cross-legged before the sill and rested my chin on my folded arms. I gazed into the darkness, the rain spattering my face. As my mind wandered, I found myself in another time, another place.

The banners of a thousand knights and footmen formed in the shadow of the Holy City's imposing walls. Their lances, pikes, and poleaxes thrust toward the sky, sunlight gleaming off pointed heads. There, among the flapping banners, shone the red standard and rampant lion of Greenshire, the green field and wolves of Woodshire, and the black-on-white hart of Whitehill. Horns and trumpets rattled in high-pitched refrain as the formation surged like a rush of water down an aqueduct.

War and battles always started thusly, all pomp and excitement. But they never ended as cleanly. Blood and death, the smell of piss and punctured bowels, grown men screaming in pain and crying for the mercy of The God—that's what awaited the soldiers. Such was the strange duality of war—humanity reduced to its worst and raised to its greatest. In a single day, a warrior might be a murderer and savior, butcher and hero. By The God, I loved it, and I prayed for forgiveness.

Thunder sounded nearby, followed by a flash of lightning. The vision swirled as the ramparts and towers of Clurak slid into the distance and faded into the night that surrounded my Thaynehold. I breathed deeply as my heart raced, remembering the surge of excitement that came with battle and the slow, grinding terror of a bivouac in the field, waiting for death.

For me, the Third Crusade had not ended well. Nor would forgiveness come.

Duke Lethon of Greenshire had dubbed me a hero, "The Savior of the Crusade," and sent me home to my family and newly granted lands. I cannot say that I was ungrateful. The lands, wealth, and status handed to me for my despicable acts had brought me and my family considerable benefits. Still, what I felt was not a hero's pride, but a murderer's shame. There were times I wished I could die, the guilt was so great.

The nightmares left me little room for questioning their intent and even less room for disagreement. The Devil had cursed me for the heinous act of murdering a Vestal. This was all I could surmise, despite the promise of redemption made by the Archbishop and his pet Duke. Perhaps the only way to keep the demon from haunting me was to cloud my mind with things more terrible and more frightening than her and those damnable eyes.

I needed to return to the Holy Land—to hold steel in my hand. To feel the rush of combat and the dread that comes from hastening to one's inevitable, violent death.

Maybe then I could forget those haunting blue eyes.

My sister saw me off when I left. It was a scene reminiscent of the last Crusade. She, in a melancholy tone, said, "Perhaps when you arrive in the land of The God, you will find the brother that left me."

Her words cut deeply. She was the only thing that had mattered to me. She was what kept me coming home, what kept me alive during the last Crusade. I wanted to find what I'd lost with her, too, though I was convinced that one's innocence could never be recovered. Her eyes were wet with tears, and her chin shook madly as she stifled the need to cry.

I'd never told her what I'd done. I never told her about the Dark Men. That truth was too sensitive—even with the person I most loved in the world. How would she feel if she knew her brother was an assassin? How was she to live with knowledge of this sort? How would I live knowing she despised me? For surely she would if she knew how many innocents I had sent to their heathen resting grounds. So I told her what I told her: The Crusade was brutal and, through skill of arms, I had brought home victory and honor to our house. It was the truth.

It was a lie.

She always sensed something was wrong, of course. Something remained untold. But she never questioned. She chose to leave me to my women, my obsessive drilling with sword and dagger, and my uncontrolled drinking. I could sense that it was difficult for her to watch me degenerate thusly. So I was not surprised when her face was not only sad and tear-streaked, but relieved when I climbed the gangplank on my way to the Holy Land.

Willem would call our liegemen in my absence. They would follow later on horse and on foot by way of the Pilgrim's Approach. It would be many months before they arrived, but I wanted to be gone.

I took my charger, armor, and kit to Greenshire and gained passage on the first vessel bound for the Holy City. I strode the same plank that had brought me home and boarded one of the old supply cogs on its daily heading for Clurak. It was an ancient thing called *The Foil* by its grim-faced captain. I wanted to reach the Duke as expeditiously as possible, I told the captain. He merely grunted, nodded, and held forth his hand for my coin. I paid him, eager in my desire to become what I once was.

I wanted to rejoin the Dark Men.

CHAPTER 2
THE VOYAGE

O n the first day of our voyage, the captain stood before the crew and announced my patronage. "We have a great personage aboard, boys," he called above the creaking ropes and wooden planking and the thumping of wind battering the single, square sail. "The Savior of Clurak has joined us for his glorious return to the Holy Land. And so, Fate must be with us!" His voice was not filled with confidence, joy or pride or awe. It dripped with sarcasm and anger.

Perhaps it was my own self-loathing and shame that made it seem so, for the crew initially cheered my arrival. A sick feeling arose in my bowels with the cheer, and I could not help but lower my eyes.

The cog was small, and I slept with my kit in the hold, my sword laying over my lap and my pack serving as my pillow. I kept my long cloak wrapped about me as a blanket, to ward off any cold from the sea. It was uncomfortable compared to my feathered-bed in the keep, but it reminded me of times past, when life was fleeting and death was ever-present. Sometimes my cloak was all that had kept me from perishing on cold, wet nights or between snow-filled mountain passes. It was strangely comforting to be held in its confines.

On the fifth day of the voyage, we passed beneath the Eastern Arch, a massive gateway under which the River Weld flowed into the great fortress city of Bannonshire. Carved in the arch's keystone was the five-pointed Star of The God.

A lump crawled into my throat as I beheld the scene. It was everything for which we'd fought, everything that represented our dominance over the Gols. Kings and priests contended for power and gold and souls. Most men struggled for survival and promises of Absolution. But Absolution was a lie, as was the promise made by the glorious walls of the city itself. The golden walls veiled the truth of its desperation: streets and ghettos choked with the poor, layered in filth and shite. Still, I joined the fight for something else.

I wanted to feel alive again.

I turned from the gate, and the city slipped by my eyes. Tall buildings, seeming to sag beneath the weight of their occupants, leaned over the waterway. Fishing piers lined the eastern bank of the river, soon giving way to culverts for tanners, smelters, and other industry to spew their waste. We passed under two pulley-operated bridges that were known as engineering masterpieces in the Northern Kingdoms. Finally, we sailed the open waters.

The Sea of Sorrows opened before us like a sheet of black porcelain. As we passed under the Western Archway, the crew let loose a great, "Ho-Ho!" and waved in the cool, sea air. They embraced the water with a lover's enthusiasm.

I could not feel the same glee, for my goal carried with it the burden of murder, the specter of fear.

The *Foil* never ventured far from the coast. The cog was not large enough to cross the Sea of Sorrows, so we bounced along the ports that rimmed the sea, stopping each ten-day to resupply with food, rum, and provisions. Because of this circuitous route, the voyage seemed to drag.

The dreams came to me. Piercing, accusing eyes and a gurgling, dying voice that whispered, "Take me home." It condemned me again and again for my crimes.

I often awoke, teary eyed and sweating. Each night the visions worsened, becoming more and more real. Images of the Nun dying on my blade banished memories of my sister and shrouded my mind as though it were a dark cloak. I took to staying awake, walking the decks at night like a phantom, listening to the snores of the crew, the hiss of the wind, the rasp of the ropes, and the creaking of the hull. It brought me a sort of peace that I cannot explain.

On the fifteenth night from Bannonshire, the beautiful city of Lyanha lay two days farther along the coast. The moon, merely a sliver of silver light, hung low on the horizon. Nights had turned cold, and I bundled against the wind, leaning on the gunwale as I fought for wakefulness. But exhaustion has a way of defeating ghosts, and I drifted to sleep.

The dream revisited me then, but it was different. It came in shades of real color, sounds, and smells. It was dark and full of menace. The falling rain rustled in the trees. The apostate woman wheezed as life slipped from her. I was there, in that bog again, visiting death upon the Nun. I pressed my knife to her skin as she heaved and groaned, coughing blood over her lips. Her eyes glazed in terror as she realized her mortality.

It is a mercy, I whispered in my sleep. As I slid the knife between her ribs, her face morphed and changed, until before me, covered in blood and sweat and muck, the face of my sister stared—but her eyes were icy-blue.

I sat straight up and called out again, "It was a mercy! It was a mercy!"

My cries reverberated along the deck, and several of the crew rose from their slumber and looked at me, wonder and fear in their eyes. I scooted back against the gunwale, pulled my cloak tighter, and shook away the horror I'd imagined.

I was cursed. The God had forsaken me. I could no longer doubt it. How else were such dreams conjured?

Those sailors I'd awakened milled together, whispering to each other. They shot me glances and crossed the Star of The God or fingered symbols of long-forgotten deities, delivering prayers into the darkness.

I looked away, toward the splintered moon that grinned back at me. I curled deeper into myself.

My eyes grew heavy, and I nearly drifted into a troubled sleep. I told myself to awaken and willed my eyes open with some success. I did not want such horrors to be visited upon me again tonight.

As I struggled with sleep, the sound of shuffling feet came to my ears. Someone was close. I peered sideways along the gunwale. A dark shadow approached.

Was I dreaming? I almost believed so, but none of the surreal terror that accompanied my dreams was present. The figure closed, and I noticed his feet were bare. It dawned on me that the crew, as superstitious as they were, was sufficiently spooked by my strange behavior and outbursts that they may move on me.

I was miserable and haunted, but I was not prepared to die. Not here. Not on this Godforsaken scow in the middle of the sea.

I moved for my knife, careful to keep it hidden beneath my cloak. I kept my head down, watching him from the corner of my eye. He was alone. I sensed no other presence, heard no others approach. The familiar but nearly forgotten feeling of impending combat crept through me, and I allowed myself a grin deep in my hood. Did this man realize he was stalking one of the infamous Dark Men of the Third Crusade? If he did, he was a fool.

For his foolishness, he would sacrifice his life.

I do not relish killing. But when a man makes to slaughter me in my sleep, I do not hesitate. Much of it, I think, is instinctual after years at war. Some, perhaps, is more human nature, though many people will flee from such a situation. To me, there must be payment in kind for an enemy who entertains such a devious desire. And as the sailor closed, I slid my legs under me, careful to keep as still as possible and my cloak casually draped.

He would go down silently, I decided with reckless arrogance. What I did not count on was an experienced killer to be aboard the cog.

Perhaps he had gained skills fighting pirate boarding parties, or he was a pirate himself at one time or a marine in one of the many navies around the Sea of Sorrows. Whatever the case, he was not what I'd expected.

When he was two paces distant, he drew a curved dirk from his belt and leaned toward my throat. It was then that I struck.

I knocked his hand aside and threw my cloak wide. I came in low and direct, keeping my elbow close to my body as I thrust with my knife. I took him by surprise, but his hesitation was short-lived. He stepped backward in a flash. My thrust did not penetrate deep enough to cut him as I was not willing to overcommit myself. He raised his blade. I smiled and waved my knife before me.

"You are a devil," he whispered. His eyes were cold—a killer's eyes.

I let a grin play across my face. "Yes, I am," I said. And I meant it. The curse had taken me. My soul, I was sure, was forfeit.

His curved knife was not effective for thrusting, so he came at me wide. I was prepared. He spun gracefully, turning a flourish in the way of the warriors on the western coasts. Doing so, he slashed downward at my throat.

I sidestepped, knocked his cut aside, and stabbed. My knife cut a trench across his ribs, sending blood spewing. I pressed the attack, lunging quickly. He was ready and pushed my hand aside. He spun and came in again. His knife scraped across my left arm, splitting my heavy quilted sleeve and cutting the skin. It was a flesh wound, but it threw off my next attack. My blade went wide. He smiled, nodded toward the bloody cut, and ran his finger across his neck as if to say, *the next one removes your head.*

Overconfidence—it is typically the mistake of youth. This man thought a minor cut was cause for bravado. I was not one to deny him his surety. I spit in his face, raised my fingers, and waved him toward me. A little encouragement provided to the weak-minded never hurts when it comes to killing.

"Come," I said. "Let us finish this."

Enraged, he wiped my spittle from his cheek and attacked. He rushed me like a fool. I had only to step aside, put out my knee, and watch as he stumbled into the gunwale. Being a sailor and accustomed to the sea, he dropped his dirk and managed to catch himself on the railing, providing me the opportunity for which I was looking.

I advanced behind him, slid my knife across his throat, and pushed his lifeless corpse over the side.

The next day, no one spoke of the missing man, and the crew became wary around me. A ten-day after the attack—more than a month on the cursed vessel in all—I watched, gargoyle-like, over the forecastle of the old cog, hoping to see the banners of Clurak in the distance or the sun glistening from the golden dome that capped the Sanctuary of the Temple of Tears.

To the port side of the *Foil*, the coast of the Holy Land slipped by for weeks, a sliver of black or brown in the distance. The salt-laden wind stung my eyes. The briny water was cold, and the smells of the sea were thick and ripe. My lips became cracked, and my cheeks chapped dry and red. I shielded my face in the crook of my arm. The Cog tossed and rolled with the waves.

I prayed to The God that the journey would end soon. One of these damnable voyages in a lifetime was more than enough. Two trips was madness, most would say, given that my so-called absolution had already been secured in the last Crusade.

Late in the voyage, the *Foil* was visited by a raven, one much like I had seen outside my keep in Rivershire. It perched on the mast above the nest. It balanced there for days, watching us with its strange blue eyes as we went about our daily routines. To the crew, it was a sort of omen. They cursed the creature. Yet, no one would drive it away.

I wondered why these people might believe in such superstitions. Were they not followers of The God? In the less civilized areas of the world, I'd heard they still found the ways of the Old Ones impossible to shirk. I wondered if this could be one of those traditions.

Whatever the case, I was glad for the beast. I found it a welcome friend—company for a soldier among sailors. Sometimes I spoke to the creature when no one was near. I must admit the bird never replied. For that, I am grateful. Then I would have known I'd gone mad. I began to take on the persona of the ominous bird, becoming aloof and hanging like a vulture waiting for the dead.

The crew continued avoiding me. Whispers followed. The men brought my mess into the hold where I'd made my bed, well away from the crew who ate on the deck in groups, who bonded through stories and dirges of the sea. At night, when sleep would not come, I sometimes sat on deck and told the strange bird about the eyes that haunted me. I shared things I would not have with another human.

The final ten-day of our voyage, I spoke to no one else, enduring the stares and whispers in silence. The second mate gave the sign of the five points, touching shoulders and hips, head and heart, in a strange effort to ward off the evil spirit that had apparently settled upon me. I slept little. When I did, I clutched my sword to my chest. There were too many dark corners and shadowy spots on the cog for safety, and the crew's strange animosity had become worrisome. The Vestal's blue eyes still visited me, though never again did I see my sister's face upon her visage.

One day, the bird disappeared.

That morning was warmer and dry. The wind pushed us swiftly, and the hearts of the men lifted. By mid-day, the sun burned high and unseasonably hot. Standing on deck, I saw a glint in the distance.

A sailor's voice rose from the nest above me, "The House of The God. I see it gleaming like the Star of The God."

A cheer rose from the crew. We had arrived.

CHAPTER 3
THE LADY ELAYNE

I was not sure how I would be received by the Duke, and so I dressed in my most courtly clothing, as it was after more than a month on a ship. I strapped my sword across my back, my knives at my waist, and adorned my warhorse with the colors of my Thaynehold. I left my armor tied in my kit and attached it to the flanks of my steed, which seemed at the time as unsteady as I. Throwing the last few personal items into my pack, I led my charger off the craft. As if to announce my arrival, my horse's shorn hooves clip-clopped on the gangplank, echoing down the causeway that opened from the pier to the inner workings of the keep.

The *Foil's* crew—with a swiftness that was unimaginable hours before—unloaded the wares that were destined for the keep and made haste to depart. I was sure my presence had caused them great consternation, and they desired to be away from me—or anywhere near me—as quickly as they might. There were other, smaller ports where they could provision. But to be so obvious seemed crass, even if understandable.

I'd killed one of their crew. They knew it and could do nothing. Say nothing.

Once on the dock, I found a bored-looking guard and sent him to find the Duke, or someone of import, and inform him the Savior had returned. I threw my pack on the boardwalk and sat upon it. I knew the Holy City well, but I had no desire to reorient myself with its mud-covered streets or take in its falsely achieved marvels. From where I sat, it looked the same, and it smelled the same, as it had a year and more ago. The only change arose from the fact that a different man occupied the Fortress Keep and a different God occupied the Temple.

Due to the sacrifices made by the Dark Men, Clurak had fallen, and now the Duke sat the throne and awaited his coronation as King of the Holy Land. The very thought of it filled me with disgust. The God had mounted His Star upon the Temple by the acts of a murderer of women.

Don't misconstrue me: I have no preference if the Temple is occupied by The God or by the heathen gods or the Old Ones. What disgusted me was the manner in which we had claimed it, the manner in which I'd delivered it unto the Archbishop. The heathen was no better to be sure, having acquired the talents of Rayfe the Betrayer to ensure the Temple remained in their hands. I just happened to be luckier that day. On any other day, Rayfe and the Vestal would have bested me. Both had been better with blades than I. The God owed His current occupation to an untimely stumble and a blade slid through a helpless woman's vitals.

A man arrived for me at the end of the dock, decorated in royal livery—the blue and white of the Holy City. An embroidered golden Star adorned the front of his tunic, and he carried a walking staff that was topped with the same Star. By the look of him, he was the Duke's valet. He bowed when he approached, though not too deeply.

I stood, returned the greeting, and said, "Ho there. I am here for the Duke." I hefted my kit to my back—the portion that was not secured to my horse—and made ready to enter the keep.

"Yes, Ser," he said. "I am to take you there directly. But first . . ." He held his hand up and clicked his fingers thrice.

Seemingly from nowhere, two boys arrived from the causeway. One secured my horse's bridle, and the other stood looking at me expectantly. Not being sure what to do, I eyed him.

"Your gear, my lord," the valet said.

"Ah. Yes," I replied and handed my kit to the boy. It was almost as big as he, and he struggled under its weight. After righting himself, he and his cohort were gone, having taken all the worldly possessions that I had brought.

"Where are they—" I started when the valet waved a hand in my face.

"To your rooms in the keep, of course, Ser," he said in that haughty tone used by nobles and their close servants. "I say again, you shall meet His Grace directly."

"Of course." I chose not to club him with the pommel of my sword for his rudeness and stupidity. "Lead on, man, with haste."

We strode through the causeway and into an arched tunnel that led below the Sorrow Wall. Atop the great stone battlement, embrasures rose and fell in the lengths between colossal round towers, where siege cannons pointed out to sea. Under the wall and into the keep, the tunnel descended. We passed beneath a raised portcullis, through an iron bound gate, and into a large bailey. I spied the servant boys split apart across the bailey. One led my charger to the stables, and the other took my gear to a series of stone buildings along the northern walls.

Ignoring them, the valet strode across the courtyard toward a large inner-gate. Two spear-wielding men-at-arms flanked it.

"This way," the valet said, and I followed like the loyal dog I was beginning to resemble.

Did the return of the man who had saved the Siege of Clurak not warrant more than some lackey collecting me as though I were a delivery of swine or pumpkins?

When we got close, one of the guards turned and pounded the knocker. The doors swung slowly, and the guards stepped forward to meet us.

"Good day," the valet said with a dismissive wave. The soldier nodded and withdrew.

We flew past the guard without fanfare, conversation, nor eye contact. We stepped inside the confines of the Holy Palace Keep, and I noticed its cleanliness immediately—as though no infection of the outside was allowed under the Duke's roof.

It is my opinion that he'd worked to separate himself from the realities of the war he waged and the filthiness of its ramifications. He had not changed, or so it seemed, since my time with the last Crusade. In the bivouac, the Duke of Greenshire had maintained the largest tent, a structure so massive it took more than five wagons to haul it. It was the transportable version of the

Bannonshire Palace, and the subject of many a jest from the boys in the field. Compensating? Arrogant? Or both?

Some commanders need distance from the grime of war to make clear decisions. Other commanders have weak hearts and take action in ignorance, thinking themselves above the throng. It is best if commanders who send other men to war should have to experience it themselves, to understand its totality. It is a thing of honor. Others have leaned on The God to alleviate them of those sorts of concerns—they find justification for their decisions in the Covenant.

I wondered what type of man the Duke was.

As I contemplated the situation before me and the proclivities of my new liege—at least while I served under the banner of the Holy City—we entered a wide hallway of polished white stone. A figure, lithe and feminine, bowed before a large set of doors that slowly closed before her. She kept her low bow until the doors slammed shut, and then she turned toward us.

I gasped. For I was sure I beheld a ghost.

Her eyes pierced my heart like a spear. For a moment, I thought I was in a waking dream, or I was asleep again, walking through an unreal world of terror. All else faded: the valet and the ridiculous expression on his face, the keep's pristine walls. Everything became nothing, except the woman.

She was clean and perfumed, not covered in slime and blood and filth as when I had last seen her. She wore an expensive dress fit for the courts here at Clurak. Her hair was dark brown, not the yellow I remembered from the bog, in the shadow of night. Here, it was braided and laced with golden thread.

But it *was* her. I could not mistake those ice-blue eyes. Surely she was a doppelganger, a devil sent here to distract me or drive me further from the blessings of The God.

Still, I refused to believe my sight. Before me stood my worst nightmares. I saw, in my mind's eye, the blood and the muck, the sheen of perspiration and rainwater glistening on her skin. I smelled her breath, her sweat, her bowels evacuating as she expired, and I tasted my own blood.

I saw her life fade. Her once bright, vibrant eyes flattened and dulled as her soul leaked into the muck.

I gasped, staggering, and reached for the wall to steady myself.

The vision stopped and looked at me, cocking her head. Her eyes lightened, deep and full of life.

"Are you alright, Ser?" she asked, her voice familiar, and yet as different as the light of the sun to the glare of the Devil's moon. But this vision *was* real. I could feel her presence, there in the castle's hall. This was no dream.

I lowered my eyes, ashamed to look upon her countenance. She reached to press a concerned hand against my shoulder, and I shied away.

"Yes, my Lady," I stammered. "A dizzy spell, nothing more. I have not slept well for weeks, having arrived yesterday from the sea."

"Ah," she said. "You must be the Savior, come to rescue us from the Ek Inir."

"Yes, my Lady. That would be me, your humble servant." I almost laughed that she would think such things. I was not here to find and kill this Ek

Inir. I only wanted to join the Dark Men. "Though the sea seems to have gotten the better of me."

"The emerald deep has proved a more worthy adversary than Rayfe the Betrayer?" she asked.

Speaking the name of my once master sent my head spinning.

"What do you know of the Darkstalker?" I asked a bit too severely. Realizing my mistake I added, "I am sorry my Lady. My exhaustion has frayed my manners to naught."

Still, I could not meet her eyes.

"It is forgiven," she said.

I nodded my gratitude, leaning more firmly against the cold stone of Clurak.

"Of course I knew the Darkstalker," she continued. "He spent much time here in the Holy Fortress—the business of war and such." She straightened and said in a gentle voice that was wrong for the face I recalled, "Be well, Ser. You look as though you've spied a phantom. You are pale, Ser, and your body shakes. Perhaps I should help you to the surgeon."

"No," I said, too harshly by thrice as she reached for me. I stepped clear of her touch.

She withdrew her hand. "Well then, Ser, I must be away, and you must regain your composure. The God be with you always." She made five points, and with that, the vision drifted into the darkness of the castle.

I was left there, alone with my phantoms and a suspicious looking valet.

"The Lady Elayne," the valet said as if expecting my question, his voice echoing down the corridor. "Her beauty can be quite fetching. She has been with us for two or three years now. Hers is a tragic story." He clucked his tongue, as if to say, *too bad, so sad,* then continued. "She lost her sister to a heathen ambush on Pilgrim's Way. She has never recovered. Poor thing. Yet, she does not end her search."

He stepped to the doors through which Lady Elayne had come, and I fell in behind him. My mind reeled. The Vestal had a sister, and I had met her. Was it coincidence or The God's cruel justice? I thought the latter and immediately wondered if I must tell her of my dark deed, if it was the right thing. How could I face her, confess that it was I who had slain her sister?

I must say that cowardice is sometimes the best option. Destroying the woman's last hope could be courage or sadism. Would I want to know if my sister—the most beloved of all I knew—were to disappear? I would want vengeance, I thought. I would slay her killer with a terrible fury. And if I were to tell Lady Elayne, would her hope not be crushed? Would her faith in The God be torn asunder? Did I have a right to do that?

Rationalization is the friend of all men, and the deepest black spot on the soul.

The valet continued, "Poor naïve girl. Her sister is, of course, dead. The heathen does not take prisoners . . ."

I looked at him, anger and sadness smoldering inside of me. I wanted to lash out and beat him about the neck and face. I wanted to grab him by his ears and slam him into the wall. What did he know of such things? What gave him right to speak of the Nun, to speak of what the Gols might have done to her? This pathetic little man spent the last Crusade lacing up shoes and tunics and fetching wine.

". . . for long," he added with a smile, having no idea what boiled inside me. He chuckled to himself. "What I mean is their prisoners don't last long! That one will not be seen again, I am sure of it."

Before I could hammer my fist into his weasel-like face, the valet threw open the massive doors, stepped to the side, and with a great flourishing bow, said, "Welcome back to the Holy Land, Savior of Clurak. With the greatest of anticipation, His Grace has awaited your arrival."

CHAPTER 4

THE ASSASSINATION ORDER

I had not seen the Duke since three years past, when I'd arrived in the Holy Land with the armies of the Northern Kingdoms. I was not disappointed. He was as mad and unfeelingly gaudy as ever.

Duke Lethan of Greenshire—soon to be the King of Clurak, the Holy Defender—was a tall man, slight of figure. He wore his golden hair long and curled at the ends, with a grandiose goatee that circled his mouth like a marmot's fur. His eyes glistened green, and his lips were hued in pink. His famous silvery plate armor—armor that was never worn in combat—girded him even here in his throne room. I supposed he needed the right clothing for the event—if he was to speak of war, he would dress for war. Pathetic, really.

I had served with the Duke as his knight at the first battle of Al' Torak. There, I had witnessed his brashness and stupidity as he sacrificed a column of knights in a mad cavalry charge against an echelon of pikemen. I had been wounded and thrown to the ground where I had lain, bleeding into the mud, for two days. It was then that I decided the life of a knight was short-lived. I belonged with the Dark Men.

Now the Duke was accompanied by two other men. One was a knight, who stood opposite the Duke. He was tall and darkly handsome for a middle-aged man. He wore a short beard and close-cropped hair. His steel plate was battered and worn, though well-tended. A mail coif hung over a chair behind him. His eyes were hard, as hard as the five-pointed white Star that adorned his black tunic. By his emblem, I fixed him a

Knight of the Holy Passage and likely a man with whom not to trifle.

He glared at me as I entered. No doubt to him, I was an honor-less turd. I nodded anyway. He returned my nod. That, at least, was promising.

The last of the triumvirate was a priest—or rather a Bishop. I surmised that he must be the Bishop of Tears, as he would be the only Bishop to serve the Holy Land on behalf of the Archbishop. He wore white robes—sweeping to the ground and rimmed in golden embroi-dery—such that he looked like a massively fat mainsail. A silver skull cap adorned with the Star sat atop his head, and a long prayer chain that ended in the Star hung from his neck. He was portly and old and wizened. A grey-white beard hung low from his chin, braided to partially dis-guise a jowly neck. His black eyes caught mine. They were cold and harder than his soft body might suggest.

The three stood in the center of a great room, merely feet apart. A golden carpet stretched from the doors to the thrones on the far side of the room. They were cut in the tall and sweeping style of the Golish Il Aruk who owned this city before we conquered it. Any other evidence of the Gols was gone, and great tapestries dangled from the ceiling, all depicting great battles of the Third Crusade and emblems of The God. The Duke reached a hand toward me and gestured.

"Come in," said the Duke.

I bowed low, flourishing my arm as wide as I could, and said, "Your Grace..." before stepping into the room.

"Welcome to the birth place of our Lord, The God." He spread his hands outward as if to encompass the world.

"Praise be to The God," the Bishop said. He performed the five-pointed ritual. The conversation stopped.

"What do you think, Savior? This is your doing?" the Duke asked when the fat man was done.

"Many died for this great fort, my lord," I said. "I was only lucky."

The knight nodded to me again, his eyes appraising. He made me nervous standing there, all steel and crust. The Duke harrumphed as though my answer was foolish.

"Let's not waste time," he said.

I was only too happy to expedite this discussion. I have little patience for talk, especially when the point may already be a forgone conclusion. And, after my experience in the hallway with that beautiful and horrifying specter, I wanted to get on with things. Even as the Duke watched, my mind kept wandering to the ghost, or the sister, or whatever she was. I needed a way to purge the fear and guilt that threatened to overwhelm me. Burying it under the fear and anxiety of battle seemed as good a way as any.

I nodded to him and said, "Yes, my lord. I seek the Dark Men. I wish to return to the rangers."

The knight glared at me.

His Grace ignored me and the disapproving look cast by his companion. "This—" He pointed a long finger at the warrior to his side. "—is Lord Commander Gavreaux, of the Holy Passage. And this is His Excellency the Bishop Tooleb of the Temple of Tears." He then signaled toward me, open palmed. "This is Thayne Aaron of Greenshire."

I bowed to each of them. And, without so much as waiting for us to introduce ourselves, the Duke moved rapidly ahead.

"The Gols and their heathen allies have formed an army. It is led, according to the Archbishop, by the Devil himself, this Ek Inir Ahn."

"So I've been told, my lord," I said. "That is why I am here. It is the fourth such Crusade," I added as though they had no understanding of history, despite the Duke being the de facto leader during the last Crusade. The Knight Commander had likely served in two of the Crusades in his lifetime and spent the rest of his days protecting the endless flow of the Northern Kingdoms' pilgrims from heathen raids.

"Their numbers are great. Too great," the Duke said. "This Crusade is different. We falsely assumed they would not campaign until summer. But the Devil makes war in the rain. We are unprepared. Their army will be upon us long before the Crusade arrives. We have called the garrisons from An Danak, and An Kolaak to defend the Holy City, but they have not yet arrived and would not be sufficient in any case.

"The Gols have defeated the garrison at Kreaak, west of Al'Torak, and are marching now on the Torak Redoubt east of the horde along the coast. If they crush that, and they will, they will have breached The Knuckles. No one will be between them and Clurak."

"Your Grace," the Knight Commander interrupted. "We are considering a course of action here that is without honor. Numbers are not what determines victory. We are warriors rife with the Spirit and Will of the The God. No heathen can stand before us. We should not stoop to assassinations and subterfuge."

"Have you forgotten, my lord," I began, "that subterfuge is what won this City? Spirit and Will are no match for steel and spear and twenty-thousand screaming heathen Gols."

"Do not insult me, assassin," The Knight Commander spit. "I have faced more than my share of steel and flesh. And I have done it standing up, blade to blade. The God protects those He favors."

I turned from him and toward the Duke. Zealots had a way of grinding my nerves. They were the reason for all this death; they were the reason for my nightmares and the destruction of my soul. Weren't they?

"Seems to me, your Grace, that the Dark Men are what is needed. A knife in the back, poison in the soup, and all that."

"The Dark Men are gone," The Duke said, without fanfare. "They are gone. Gone away."

"Gone?"

"Yes. I disbanded them. Once we had taken the Holy City. Sadly, you are all that remains."

"I see." I tried to keep my face flat, but the madness of his statement seemed unreal. The Dark Men disbanded? Or executed? I would avoid that uncomfortable thought.

In times like these, special men with special skills were needed. What did this mean for me? For my redemption? Was I destined to die in some meaningless charge or melee in a field of shite, one of many, faceless dead? It had been a long trip to pick up sword and shield and plate to die en masse. It was not what I had hoped. I did not belong on the field with the regulars. But, if that was the Duke's plan, then why had I been singled out and brought here?

"Yes," he said. "I had no more use for thieves and murders at the time. And after the issue with the Darkstalker, I had reason to fear for my life—and for their loyalty. Present company excepted of course."

At least he had our measure correctly.

"But, you do now," I ventured.

"Uh . . . yes. I do," he said. And with no further ado, he added, "I need you to murder this Ek Inir—this General of theirs."

The Knight Commander started. "Your Grace. Honor and The God dictate that we not become murderers. That is the way of the heathen—"

The Duke cut him off with a wave of his hand. "You have had your piece, Commander."

"It is not dishonorable to slay devils," interjected the Bishop, his jowls jiggling as he spoke. "The taking of their lives is cleansing of The God's world. Forget not, the rumors of this undefeatable, cursed warrior that guard him and his pet Sorcerer. His death would be welcomed by The God as well. It is said the phantom cannot die."

I looked at the Bishop quizzically and cocked my head. He merely smiled at me, though there was little warmth. Cursed warrior? I wanted some elaboration, but the Duke continued on his agenda.

His Grace nodded grimly. "I care little about superstition and rumor, your Excellency. Kill the Ek Inir, Ser Aaron. That is the singular mission. And, it goes without saying . . ."

"We never discussed this," I finished his sentence. "I must prepare, your Grace."

It was war. I understood that. But to have the soon-to-be-King of the Holy Land stand before me and disavow his oaths of honor, made to The God, was disconcerting, even with the support of the Temple. Sure he had sanctioned the use of the Dark Men, but never in the murder of another Noble, even a heathen one. Would we abandon the traditional ways of victory and draw noble blood? It seemed dirty, or something worse.

When I was with the Dark Men we had slain officers, engineers, and messengers, or done deeds to terrorize populations, poisoning wells and food supplies. But we had never outright assassinated a noble. In the end, was there a difference? Perhaps I was a fool. Perhaps these were akin to the Duke's conversations with Rayfe—the once leader of the Dark Men turned Betrayer—before I had dispatched him.

Regardless of the genesis of this mission, murder was something at which I excelled. It was a skill I had honed in the last Crusade. To be sure, I was out of form from a year spent softly in my keep, but I knew how to kill from the shadows. That is not something one ever unlearns.

A thrill ran the length of my spine. The Dark Men may not be alive and well, but I was back in the match. I had come to purge myself of the demon that haunted my nights, and killing Gols was how I would do it. Killing the master of their army would only make it easier. Perhaps this would allow me to find peace. Perhaps this would allow me to forget those eyes that yet plagued me so.

I nodded and bowed.

The Knight Commander sneered at me; a savage smile spread across his face. I felt compelled to step away from this dangerous man.

"The Bishop says to not fear Retribution from The God. Acts such as these are not murder. You are cleansing the world of the Devil's right hand. He—this general—is a monster as true as a drake or demon." The Commander bowed to the Duke and began to retreat from the room. Once he was at the door, he turned once more and said, "But, I am not sure I agree with his Excellency. Be careful of your soul, Dark Man. It is nearly lost. This murder may be its undoing."

CHAPTER 5

THE PREPARATION

My sleep was not easy in coming. I had been put into the outbuildings so I might leave without being seen. Normally, I would have begun my journey that night, but the voyage had left me exhausted. Still, I could not sleep.

Thoughts of my mission spun unabated through my imagination. They always did before a mission, but this was different. I remembered things, distasteful things, from the last Crusade. I thought of Elayne and her sister and that night in the bog only a few days' ride from here. I thought again of my decision to kill the woman. Driven by mercy, I had taken her life. Was it mine to take?

She had said, "Take me home."

I had done that, hadn't I? I had freed her. If not, I had meant to, and that should be good enough.

These are things that trouble a man who was raised a knight, bound to a certain code. These are things that also trouble a righteous man. And they had troubled me since I had put survival before honor and joined the Dark Men. With the murder of the Nun, I had fallen headlong into depravity, and now I was a ghost of my former self.

I sat up in bed and leaned my head into my hands. *I must get gone*, I remembered thinking. I belonged where my mind would not wander to things I could not change, terrible things that I had done.

Something shifted in the room, and I peered into the darkness. My hand found my dagger, which I kept under my pillow, and I slid it into my lap. I saw nothing at first, but when the noise came again, I spun my head. Two piercing ice-blue eyes drilled into me from the dark. Was the Vestal Nun there, come to take me?

I gasped and pulled myself up on the bed. The movement must have spooked the creature. I heard the flap of wings and the caw of a raven. It shot through the open window and into the night.

I could not sleep after that. I penned a short missive to my sister and left it on my tiny writing desk where it would be found, my seal pressed into the wax. It was nothing of import, just to let her know I yet lived. I dressed, committed now to leaving on my mission early. I wore my studded leathers and left my plate in the room. I strapped my longsword on my hip and my long-knife opposite. I slipped two more knives into my boot-sheaths. Pulling on my gloves, I secured my heavy cloak and threw open the door.

A figure stood there and loomed into the room. It was slight but menacing in the dark.

"Stay your hand, Thayne," the figure said, and I immediately recognized it as Elayne's. "We should have words."

I released my knife but did not immediately move from the door. What would bring the woman to my quarters this late at night? Outside, it had started to rain, and clouds darkened the moon. A chill breeze rolled into the room.

"A lady coming to a man's room at this hour should be frowned upon," I said. "Your reputation is at risk, my lady. I hope you took precautions."

"Let me in, Ser. We must speak of my sister. I believe you have seen her, Edweene." I heard the frown in her voice, even if she masked it on her face. Her eyes welled with unshed tears.

"Who—" I started to ask.

"No one told me. I divined it myself after our encounter. You were most disturbed by my presence. I must say, I don't usually have that effect on people."

"My lady," I began, my head lowered. "I must apologize, for I knew not your relation until after we met." I moved aside, my heart pounding like a drum. What would I tell this woman? What would I want someone to tell my sister if I had been murdered? "Please, come in. Though I am sure these quarters are not to your apartment's standards."

"You are a Thayne, are you not?" She removed her cloak and gloves and tossed them on my disheveled bed.

"Yes, my lady. Thayne of Rivershire, in—"

"I know of it," she said. "Awarded for your courage."

My gut twisted. She knew. I had killed her sister in the most cowardly manner and been rewarded for it. It was almost too much to bear.

"I am told so, yes." I almost choked on the words.

She sat in the chair at my writing table, keeping her eyes on me—those piercing, convicting eyes. I made great effort not to look into them as I stood before her. She looked down for a moment. Her hands played across the desk and picked up the small package I had left there. She read for a moment then turned to me.

"Your sister or wife?" she asked.

"Sister."

"And how would she feel if you were missing and someone knew of your demise but was not telling?"

"My lady," I started to defend myself, but there was no defense. To be sure, I had not known there was a relation. I hadn't even known the woman's name, but I had slain her in the worst of conditions. Worse, I had left her body there in the mud, alongside Rayfe the Betrayer. "If I had known—"

"Do not fool yourself, Ser, and certainly do not try to fool me," she spoke in a strong voice, keeping it as steady as she might. But I heard the crack there that spoke of barely contained emotion, as though she would break down if she showed the slightest weakness. "There were rumors of her capture, of course. And so, I have not hoped for some time. If truth be told." She paused and turned to gaze over the broken fields east of the city.

"I felt her soul depart," she said through misty eyes.

I nodded to her in silence, lacking any meaningful words. I watched as the city lights and lanterns flickered and danced like fireflies. It was quiet and solemn as a corpse. I felt my heart breaking. I wanted to hold her, apologize, and beg her forgiveness.

She broke the stillness. "My sister was saved by you, Aaron. The God has whispered this to me." She rotated toward me and looked me straight in the eyes. "Her immortal soul, imprisoned by the Gol Sorcerers, was released by you. You must have felt it, too."

She was demanding that I agree, but I could not confirm her delusions. I had been there. I had slid the knife through her sister's ribs and sent her home. But where was home? Had her soul left her, or had I denied it any resting place, either here on earth or in the coming world? I had felt nothing of her soul as I murdered her. How could I? It was hers to feel, not mine. But at that moment when I destroyed this most beautiful of creatures, I knew that my soul, which had been withering away for years, had perished.

I nodded to her, one tilt of the head. It was confirmation enough. It had to be as it was all I could stomach. I, the Savior of Clurak had also saved her sister's soul—a lie. This was how history was written—to the victor goes the glory, be it true or not.

My knees wobbled and I nearly staggered, catching myself with a hand against the wall. She knew it was a falsehood, but she needed it. It was all I could give her. She smiled at me, her eyes living and bright and full of gratitude, tears streaking her face.

It was too much.

I fell to my knees before her and begged her forgiveness, begged for redemption. But she could give me nothing. It was for me to find on my own.

The last thing I felt of her was her hand slipping softly through my hair as she stood. She picked up her cloak and gloves and disappeared into the night.

I collapsed to the floor and sobbed.

CHAPTER 6
RAIDERS

I left before the sun rose. Clouds rolled in from the sea, and I felt the faint sensation of rain in the air. Back home, rain brought life and joy and smelled clean and full of promise. Here in the Holy Land, the rain smelled of mold and decay, a promise of an early death or toil at someone else's behest.

The raw pain of last night's lie remained with me, and I did my best to ignore the bone-deep dread. I roused the livery boy and saddled my horse. After I loaded my bedroll and gear on the beast, I thanked the boy and made my way toward the bailey gate. I walked, leading my steed and trying to be as silent as possible. I sure as hell didn't want to wake anyone. The whole point was to get gone, and to do so quietly in the morning dark.

Rain fell as I headed to the gate. The deluge was good for me, perhaps not this early in the exploit, but if it held it would provide me cover for my eventual raid. I mused to myself that in the Holy Land, downpours did not give life, but brought death—covered the advance of enemies, hid the dust trails of flanking cavalry, dampened sound, and made infiltrators difficult to detect. It denied archers their advantage and provided a useful noise to drown the dying cries of my targets.

Rain was my friend. I did not curse it; I welcomed it.

I pulled my hood over my face, hoping to keep the wetness from my hair and eyes. I walked in silence, my boots slipping and sliding in the rapidly worsening mud. I steadied myself with my charger's bridle and made sure to progress carefully. It was as if I had never left: the rain falling, the wetness of the landscape, the foreboding of a coming mission. I breathed in the morning air and felt it cool my insides.

I was home, I thought. I had come home. The realization frightened me more than anything. Would I ever be able to find peace without violence?

As I contemplated my situation, a dark figure loomed from the night, mere paces in front of me. I startled and pulled up short, my hand instinctively drawing my long-knife and readying it before me, blade pointed.

The figure spoke in deep, masculine tones I recognized immediately as the Knight Commander. "Ho," he said. "I do not come to attack you. Only to talk."

"The talking is done, my lord," I said. "His Grace has dispatched me on this perilous mission." I tried to sound stark and full of import. Truth was, the knight put the fear of The God into me. I took a step back, freeing up space between us in case it came to blows.

"Tell me the real reason you do this," he said. His voice echoed through the bailey. This was not a man who worried about being quiet.

"Please, Ser," I said. "Your voice—it carries." He nodded apologetically, and I added, "I have come for the Crusade, as I have made clear."

"Nay. I think not," he said smugly, his voice lower now. "You seek redemption, my lord, or forgiveness. It is written on your face. Anyone who looks can see it, plain as the rain. Something inside ails you."

How could he know of my tortured spirit? How could he know of my broken soul?

"And, what if I did?" I asked. "The God—your God—has cursed me with terrifying dreams and haunting visions. I cannot continue living like this. I must find rest from this nightly dread." I immediately regretted giving him any indication that he was correct in his assessment. I would give him no more.

"I think you are looking in the wrong place," he said and tapped his heart. "Look here." He grasped his tunic where the Star of the God was embroidered and added, "And look here. You can find what you need. More murder is—"

I changed the direction of the conversation. "Your premise is flawed, Lord Commander. I don't seek forgiveness or redemption. I seek only to forget."

"Forget what? Killing? Death? It is laughable, man. You will never forget what you did here. Your burden is to accept. Another assassination—"

"By killing this man, we can stop the war before it begins," I interrupted, wanting to be done with him. "Is one murder worth that?"

"You are a fool, then. This war is coming. Your sword in the Devil's back cannot stop it. You can only hope to delay it. Mark my words: if you murder this Golish heathen, when the war *does* come, it will rise with the vengeance of the damned. The Gols will not forgive such a thing. And their conversion to The God will be difficult indeed." He let that sink in for a moment, as if I cared.

What import is conversion? Trading one overlord for another?

"I do not condone what you and the Duke do here." He went quiet, thoughtful for a moment. I supposed he was done with his lecture. I grabbed the saddle horn and made ready to mount when

he added, "Nor will I impede it. But remember
this, my lord, murder is not the way to redemption. Murder is not the way to true victory—in this
or any war."

I stared him in the eye and scoffed. "One
knight's murder is another's glory." That was the
truth as I saw it. I pulled myself into my saddle
and said, "Good morning, Ser."

Avoiding the Lord Commander's eyes, I rode
through the bailey gate and into the darkened
streets of the Holy City. The sun would rise soon,
and I wished to be free from the city walls by then.
I spurred my horse into a trot and moved along
the cobbled streets at a much faster pace. I was
sacrificing silence for speed, but I didn't want any
would-be spies to catch me in the light of day.

I rode through the palace district that bor-
dered the keep, passed protected gates and
courtyards, and exited through the gateway that
separated those with money and power from
those without. Outside was the market district,
centrally located and filled with the wide, empty grounds of the bazaar and the closed shops
of newly-minted merchants. Through the sec-

ond gate, I entered the warehouse district, which spanned the city's breadth. To the north, the district ended at the docks, and the streets were wide to allow for the passage of merchandise and trains of wagon and horse. To the east, I would find the shanties—where those of less than wealthy means made their homes. But I turned south and made my way to the main gate.

The place had changed since I was there last—the new regime had ousted all of the heathen merchants and replaced them with shops and merchant warehouses from northern sellers and speculators. The population would not take that well, I figured. I supposed it was the nature of conquest, as foolish as it may be. It seemed to me that having a friendly population at one's back would be invaluable in a time of siege. But I was no king, so what did I know.

At last, the South Gate—the city's main thoroughfare—yawned before me. The sun began to rise over the eastern horizon, casting muted rays of yellow into the dreary, wet landscape. It was beautiful in its own way, a recognition that suffering and pain and sorrow existed even under the light of The God. Ahead, two guards stood at the gate, their spears held upright at rest position. High above the portcullis, flanked by the two massive towers that protected the barbican, I spied the raven. It sat, its blue eyes fixed on me, mirroring my movements. I wondered what it meant. Was there some Sorcerer that studied me through the creature's eyes, or was it a manifestation of my own dark soul?

As I approached the gate, the guards waved me past without a word. Soon, I found myself on the Wide Road—the path that spanned the western portion of Holy Land. The Wide Road, and its eastern counterpart The Pilgrim's Approach, allowed for commerce to thrive between the cities, towns, and forts within its rather porous borders. More importantly, the road made possible the rapid movement of men-at-arms and supplies.

But in the rain, the way became choked with glue-sticky mud. Wagon wheels would not find good purchase, and horses and men alike would quickly tire and slow from fighting against it.

With the morning's rain, I had already begun to feel the exhausting effects of the mud on my horse's stride and chose to ride at a leisurely pace. I had no definitive time in which to accomplish my mission—the Duke had said, 'as soon as practical'—and harming my mount for a day's savings would be foolish.

I rode in silence, the raven as my companion. It flew from tree to tree, rock to rock, always keeping me in sight, but distant enough from my physical being to prevent capture or killing with my little-used bow. I played a game with it, guessing where it would land next. Its presence became important to me, occupying my mind, keeping it from drifting to topics and memories best kept cordoned from my mission.

The Duke's scouts had reported the Gol's encampment far to the west, so I didn't expect anyone to be out in force. But if war was coming to Clurak, there would be spies.

The road was flanked on either side by sweeping hardwoods with hanging moss. Water-logged fens intermittently covered the ground, and thick brush choked the areas between. It was a perfect place for an ambush, and it was near the place where I had faced Rayfe the Darkstalker. I was on guard, hand on my sword, eyes scanning the foliage for would-be attackers. It was not necessary, for the day ended with me having seen no one, except the occasional traveler or merchant.

As night fell, I had passed several small villages and a group of spearman at a checkpoint, but had not made as much progress as I'd hoped. I had expended much time and energy due to the rain, and my increased attentiveness to every noise I heard or traveler I met. I decided it would be wise to continue before resting.

As I rode, the rain continued to fall, though now it became a thin drizzle that shrouded the air like a fog. With the coming of darkness, it felt like I was swimming through a dream, the edges of which were fuzzy and confining. The rain stopped, the fog thickened, and within a span, my ability to see more than a few paces was severely curtailed. It was time to make camp.

I had not seen the raven in hours, and I was happy. The creature, once a welcome distraction, was starting to become disconcerting.

It was cold. My joints ached, and I was exhausted from two nights with nearly no sleep. So tired was I, that I chose to forego a fire. I hobbled my horse, removed the saddle, and made camp in a thicket of hardwood and scrubby ferns. The woods were thick, and I was well out of eyesight of the road. I unpacked my bedroll, placed my sword beside me and my long-knife under the leather of my saddle, which I used as a pillow. Pulling my bedroll and cloak about me, I readied myself for a few hours of shuteye.

Sleep came easily at first, the insects and night-birds lulling me into a sort of trance that ushered in my slumber. I drifted away, and my conscious mind faded to a smudgy darkness. Then the dream came, an expected, if unwanted visitor. In it, I leaned over the girl and watched her, listened again to her beg me, "Send me home." Her eyes drilled into me, desperate, as though she meant to tell me something. Her bloody, frothing mouth formed the word, "Home," but the sounds that came out were completely different.

"Wake, now!" the voice said.

I awoke with a thundering heart.

Silence in the woods was my first indication that I was not alone. It was a wonder I could hear anything over the pounding in my chest. I calmed myself with deep breathing and focused concentration. I heard four of them at least—one in each of the cardinal directions. Instincts, long unused, took control of my body, and I rose to a short crouch. I picked up my sword in my right hand and slid my long-knife from under the pillow with my left. I was rusty for sure. The joints in my arms were clunky, and my knees and back creaked and popped. It seemed like anyone could hear it for leagues in the silence of the night. It was downright incredible how much ability one loses in a year. Training in the bailey was no replacement for action in the field to keep me sharp and in shape. I hoped the time away would not result in my untimely demise.

I was about to find out.

CHAPTER 7
THE FIGHT

M emories of a fight in these same bogs rushed upon me. That particular struggle had not ended well, with three of my compatriots dead, and my once-leader, Rayfe, betraying us all. I vowed this night would not be the same. I slinked into the thick ferns and brush on the side of my campsite, careful not to spook my horse. There, I waited.

My enemies were fast and good at their craft. If I'd been in the open, I would have been dead, feathered full of arrows or pointy-headed javelins. The thick woods gave me a little advantage. I meant to use it. They were quiet, but not as silent as they should have been. Judging from the sound, the one to the south was the farthest. He had the most difficult stalk, for his route took him mostly through water. He would be tired when he fell upon me.

Hopefully, I'd be finished with the others by then.

I moved and hunkered down on the south side of my camp, disguised among the heavy underbrush. It was my best bet for surviving an attack by four trained assassins. The ground was soaked, and I'd be hard pressed to find good traction. I would have to be careful.

The first assassin came from the woods directly in front of me. He must have exited directly from the road, as he was far ahead of the others. He was hunched and wore dark leathers, a black hood, and a mask covering his face. By his dress, he was a Golish cutthroat. I'd faced his likes before. He moved lightly across the ground, his foot barely touching the earth before he put the next one forward. In the night, he was almost invisible; if it wasn't for a slice of moonlight, I might not have spotted him as easily. He crept upon my bedroll with his curved knife drawn, apparently unaware that I had foiled their surprise.

As he slid toward my bedroll, I drew back and flung my dagger. I watched is it soared, end over end, in a gleaming arc that took him in the neck. He spun sideways and released a loud gurgle that echoed through the stillness. He dropped to the ground with a muffled *thunk* and rolled, hands grasping and scratching at his throat. The wound pumped blood over the ground.

Anxious to stop the noise, I bounded to him and split open his head with my broadsword. He stopped rolling and gurgling after that, but the damage was done. There was no doubt the others knew I was on my guard.

The second heathen came from the east, while I was still removing my blade from the dead man's skull. The assassin saw me, hesitated for a fraction of a breath, and rushed. He used a spinning attack, some kind of wild looking whirlwind of arms and blades. I dodged from one as the second fell on me. I was barely able to deflect it with my sword, and he struck with his other hand. I stepped aside, swiping with my off-hand and sweeping the weapon. He was open now, and I recognized fear in his eyes.

I thrust forward with my sword, meaning to end it. But he was fast. He dodged sidelong, and my blade missed his heart, sliding through the left side of his abdomen. I felt his leather tunic give way, then the muscle peel aside and the kidney too, before the blade tore through his flank. He lurched, clutching at the wound, and I drove my knife through his eye. He fell forward and expired.

I could not get the weapon free, as it was lodged in the man's destroyed eye socket, so I let it go as he collapsed. I twisted to the west, in the direction of my next assailant, and went into my fighting stance. I gripped the pommel of my broadsword with two hands and held it above me, point aimed at the sky. From this position, I could cleave or parry. The weapon was too heavy to hold perpendicular to my body for too long, so this was the best position I could maintain for more than a few short moments.

I didn't have to wait long. The assassin loomed out of the darkness, silhouetted against an empty spot between two trees.

This killer was smarter than the others. He pulled up short and slung a knife at me. Not expecting it, I spun to the side, barely in time, but not before the blade sizzled across my shoulder. It left a swath of blood and ruined flesh.

I roared and rushed him.

I covered the ground in no time, my sword cleaving toward his neck. He shifted to the left and retreated. My blade swept down and missed, but I shouldered into him and drove him backward. He was a slight man and did not resist the charge well. My fury flung him into a thick oak, where he slid to the ground. As he recovered from the blow, I drove my blade through his heart.

As I dispatched him, steel cut my leather-clad back. I had leaned down to administer the death blow, and that caused my attacker to narrowly miss a killing strike. Still, the blade split the armor and left a shallow slice across my shoulder blades. I spun sideways to face my attacker as he took another swing. This time the blade crossed my upper thigh, splitting the skin and muscle like an orange. I could not stop from crying out. I stumbled past him, struggling to keep my balance.

Knowing he would take the opportunity as I went by, I chose to throw myself on the ground and roll. Luckily, he did not expect my maneuver, and his slash went high. If I had continued my stumbling, he would have killed me for sure.

I was nearly helpless as he closed to finish it. I raised my sword in a futile effort to parry and watched as his scimitar descended. I closed my eyes.

His steel crashed through my parry, forcing me to release my weapon. After destroying my last defense, he raised his curved blade. I saw triumph in his eyes. Part of me was glad of it. My torment would end tonight, in this fitting place. He brought the blow down again, but the strike never came. Instead, my attacker emitted a hollow grunt and fell, his weight crushing me and his blade spilling into the bog.

It took me a moment to realize what had happened, that I had been saved. When I did, I rolled his body off of me and leaped to my feet. I picked up my sword and scanned the darkness for my defender.

Everything went silent. The sliver of moonlight disappeared behind rain clouds, the darkness suddenly complete. In the trees, two tiny blue eyes glowed. I gasped. The damn demon bird still watched me. It was unsettling.

That, in itself, was strange enough, but, who had helped me? There was not another soul present. The question hung in my mind, unanswered.

I staggered, wounded and bleeding, to squat in the grass and rushes, the bodies of four dead, Golish assassins around me. I needed to rest, but I also needed to get gone. The enemy would come again. And death drew death.

The corpses would call savage animals and scavengers. I rolled them into the swamp and picked up my camp. I wasn't sure how far I could make it tonight with my wounds, but I needed to move. I decided to go as far as my body would allow, then I would stop and consider the implications of this battle—and sleep. I had to sleep.

Two conclusions that I drew from this fight nagged at me as I took my breather. One, somehow, the heathens had known I was coming, and two, someone had rescued me. I had no idea why.

CHAPTER 8

THE LYCH
REVEALED

The mission was already over as far as I could tell. Any hope of surprise had dissipated when it became clear the enemy's assassins had followed me from the Holy City. How could I hope to dispatch their leader when he knew I was coming? He'd have his guards tightened and alert like a Bannonshire Lord warding his daughter's innocence.

A smarter man would have abandoned the mission—made for higher ground. But I am not usually the smarter man. I came to the Holy Land for a reason, and the only way I could free my eternal soul, or even to achieve a modicum of peace from my torment, was to do what I must.

If I died, so be it. My pain would be over.

Before I could think about how to murder this Golish noble, I had to find a place to rest and heal, for a short while at least. I rode along the Wide Road, still heading west and fully aware that I was wide open, ripe for ambush. I was in too much pain to allow my horse to ride across country, however, so I risked staying on the road.

I hunched in the saddle, each stride of the horse driving pain up my leg and into my brain. Several times I almost fell, and I wondered if I would make it much farther. All the while, I felt as though someone was tracking me, watching me. These invisible eyes burned into my back and into my mind. I often looked behind me or scanned the trees. Sometimes, I would stop after rounding a corner and watch for followers. But always there was nothing. My fear was slowing my advance too much, and I forced it away, ignoring the persistent worry.

The sun drifted lazily upward behind a jagged wall of clouds that seemed to linger forever. With the coming of the muted sun, the rains returned. I cursed my luck and directed my steed from the road. I had ridden as far as I would today, and now I needed to rest.

Into the bog I headed again, until I found a high, flat spot above the marsh. Large, twisted trees rose about the place, forming a sort of thicket with moss and vines overhanging into a makeshift roof. Little rain pierced the canopy. I unsaddled my horse and removed my bedroll, laying it on a dry spot.

Once I had tended to my horse, I sat and started on my wounds. I scrubbed them with what clean water I had remaining. Then, using thread that all experienced soldiers kept in their kits, I sewed the wounds shut. It was awfully painful and it wasn't much, but it would have to do. Later, if I could find some salacweed, I would treat the wounds to reduce infection and speed healing. But that was low on my list of things I needed to handle.

Though my wounds were not life-threatening in a normal situation, my world was far from normal. I was in the woods with no surgeon or priest and no clean water. It was raining, and I was filthy. Infection could set in at any moment, and I was weak and in terrible pain. Even death seemed a mercy to me.

All day as I had ridden, eyes were on my back. I was haunted by the feeling that someone watched. Imagination had a way of killing, and determining what was imagination and what was real could mean the difference between life and death when facing an enemy as devious and skillful as mine. But after having circled the perimeter of my camp and finding no sign of attacker or spy, and seeing no sign of the raven, I determined that my paranoia was getting the best of me. I was seeing phantoms.

Once my camp was set and I had put out the small eating bowl from my kit to gather rain water, I laid down and set my head on the leather of my saddle. Rolled up in my cloak and bedroll, I pushed all thought from my mind. I needed sleep. I hoped that my blue-eyed demon would let me rest tonight. Thus far today I had escaped her condemnation, the pain and suffering pushing her from my thoughts, just as I had hoped.

With the coming of sleep, the opportunity to haunt me would arrive for the ghost. Considering my reduced resilience from exhaustion and injury, now would be a good time for the phantom to drive me, headlong, over the edge of sanity.

I went to sleep filled with worry and self-doubt.

When I awoke, it was dawn's dark, the coming of morning. Rain pounded on the canopy of leaves, trees, and vines, leaking through in dips and drabs to drench me and my kit. I shivered.

I had slumbered too long. I stood, the soreness in my leg and side tearing so badly I almost fell. I could not suppress the loud groan that echoed in my little thicket and shot into the night. Tomorrow would come soon, and I wanted to have reached the Golish bivouac by then. I saddled my charger after having made sure he'd fed and drank water. Once he had, I led him from the cover of the wood and into the deluge.

The rough ground was dangerous for his fragile legs—the smallest hole or stone could lame the beast--so we moved slowly through the bog until we reached the road. It was a mess of muddy slop and deep ruts of clay-like track, laid down by merchants and refugee alike. Several lonely figures walked, heading east toward the safety of the Holy City—refugees from the massacres I was sure had occurred at the hands of the Golish horde.

I shook my head in sadness and would not meet their hollowed eyes as they trudged. This was not their fight, yet they suffered the greatest.

The presence of the war torn emigrants told me I was getting closer to the front. I would have to weigh wariness against the impending need for swiftness. Caution won few battles, but it provided the root for aggressive action when it was necessary. I would need both in abundance when the time came.

I mounted up, careful to put as little pressure on my wounded parts as possible. I swept into the night, moving as quickly as I could without endangering my horse.

Toward the end of the day, I crossed the River Rak. I had been here once before, in pursuit of the apostate Nun and Rayfe the Darkstalker. It was within a league of where I was that I had faced them for the final time and saved the siege of Clurak from failure. It was a place filled with terrible memories. It represented the loss of my soul, the abandonment of all my beliefs.

I chose not to rest that night and urged my horse, putting as much space between me and the river as possible. I camped far from the water's edge and allowed myself a few hours of shuteye that morning.

I rode and camped for two more days, the invisible watcher ever-present. My nights were short, as my wounds, and my nagging need to get on with the mission, seemed to conspire against my desire for slumber. It continued to rain each day and each night, alternating between a heavy deluge and a solid misty drizzle. It was overbearing, as though I carried a heavy, wet blanket over me at all times. It was claustrophobic, as though my life was closing in around me.

To make it worse, the never-ending stream of refugees continued. Their sad, depressed presence moved against me, like the current in a thick, slow river of shite. I could not get on with this murder soon enough.

On the second day from the river, I passed the ruins of Al' Torak. They peeked above the landscape to my right. Their blackened stone walls were shattered husks of the mighty Golish fort that had once stood, protecting the inlet of the River Rak from invasion from the Sea of Sorrows. Now, the great fortress was naught but a black skeleton in the night, a testament to both the futility of war and the permanence of its destruction.

It was said to be haunted by the warriors who had died that day defending its palisades. They had perished, by all accounts, honorably, standing to the end. But the Crusaders in the First Crusade had been merciless. History said that no man, woman, child, or livestock from the fort, or the once-thriving town below, had survived that siege. Perhaps the ghosts of the peasants also remained there, for they had suffered the worst.

If anyone, they were the ones with unfinished lives.

The road took me another two days before I knew I was close. The lines of refuges had thinned. Signs of skirmishes could be seen here and there, and columns of smoke wafted in the distance. I left the road and went into the wood. When I found a good place for a rest, I stowed my kit and made my camp. It was still morning, so I moved ahead to scout.

It wasn't long before the woods thinned and the smoke drew close enough to smell. I tethered my horse. The rain had ceased. If history held, it would only be hours before it started again.

I crouched in the deep rushes and ferns. Ahead of me, the bog and its mossy hardwoods parted, giving way to scraggly twisted trees that popped among round, moss-covered rocks. The landscape was difficult and rugged, the ground soft, if not actually covered in water. A league or more ahead, several hundred columns of smoke drifted languidly upward to meld with the rainclouds.

The briny odor of the sea drifted to me from the north. Far beyond, rising from behind the horizon to the southwest, a thick column of black smoke tumbled into the sky. That would be the Kreaak Garrison crushed and burned to the earth by the invading Gols. If I was not successful here, the Torak Redoubt would share the same fate.

By the sheer number of watch fires, I gathered the army to be close to twenty-thousand or more. The Holy City would have no chance against such a host, despite the claims of Knight Commander Gavreaux and the depth of his zealotry. In due time, a score more villages would fall, and then the Holy City itself would be toppled by the Golish horde. There was no possibility that the Crusade would arrive by then.

I could not—would not—allow innocents to fall beneath the boots of either Gol or Crusader. If my knife could spare these peasants that stood in this host's path even a day of the mayhem, rape, and death that followed a marching army, my own conception of honor demanded that I must. My blade would find its target.

I felt invigorated as I considered the heroic implications of my intent. Perhaps such a thing could purge the terrible things I had done—the lies, the murder, the subterfuge—from my heart. Perhaps one could restore their honor with murder.

I slunk from the brush, wanting a better look at the encampment, reconnaissance being critical for infiltrations such as mine. Walking, as I was, with a wounded leg and side made reaching a distance from the camp from which I could watch a painful undertaking. I hid on a high, tree-covered mound, surrounded by rounded rocks. Before me, the badlands of rock and twisted trees ended and spread into a long, open field. Several hundred paces distant, a forest of tents and weapons stacked in neat little triangles started. The watch-fires extended as far as I could see. Hundreds of banners hung atop standards throughout the camp.

I was mistaken in my initial calculations, I realized. This army numbered beyond twenty thousand—twice what I'd guess. I let loose a low whistle.

"It will be a massacre, if I allow this to happen," I heard myself speak under my breath.

How could the Gols grow and recruit this army, and the Archbishop and Duke be so far behind? It must be all the Golish nobles from Gol Toran. The Crusade needed time to face an army such as this. Was the Duke's reconnaissance so poor, or his spy networks so ineffective, that he could allow an army of this size to form on his border? It was incredible incompetence to me. If he had but allowed the Dark Men to survive, he would have known.

The Gols had set pickets surrounding the encampment, a hundred paces or so from the closest tents. They circled the camp, standing with spears set in the ground and watching into the darkness. They were undisciplined though, unafraid of whatever faced them. It was at once a demonstration of their strength and a tribute to their arrogance. This sloppiness was what would mark the death of their leader, I swore.

The tents were set haphazardly, groups of twenty or thirty surrounding a central tent, above which flew the standard of a Golish Lord—here a bear's head, there a mad-looking dog or lion, there a large-toothed fish. A circuitous, snake-like series of pathways wound between the watch-fires. Around the entire affair, a makeshift battlement had been formed of wicked spikes and wooden ramparts.

The bivouac was immense and awe-inspiring. I had not seen such a gathering of warriors since the Third Crusade sprawled in the shadow of Clurak. At the center of the encampment, three large tents rose like bright-colored canvas palaces. Above them flew two enormous banners: a giant red dragon on a field of white and a coiled black serpent on yellow.

One of those must be the Ek Inir's tent. I had seen what I needed to see. I backed out of my position and returned to my horse. From there I returned to my camp. I had a lot to consider tonight.

I had expected things to be hard, but these circumstances pitted me against the impossible.

Chapter 9
The Assault

I arrived in my camp late in the evening. I would rest there tonight and the following day. I would go into the camp tomorrow evening, well after sunset when the heathens would be most unprepared.

I sat in my camp and contemplated the situation. Gnawing on a piece of hardtack, I began to formulate a plan. But every time I came close to finalizing one, a complication arose in my mind, and I discarded it. More than a little frustrated, I sat back and stared at the sky. The clouds had parted for a brief moment, and I made out the stars for the first time in several nights.

Was it an omen? Perhaps I should abandon this foolish quest and return home. Would it bring dishonor on me? On my family? My sister had hoped I could find the old me here in the Holy Land. I had not said as much, but I knew he was dead. He would never return. I had seen too much, done too much. I wondered if my sister, the Lady of Rivershire, looked upon the same stars. I wondered if she thought of me, even as I thought of her.

As I remembered better times, before I was cursed with the memories given me by The God and his damnable Crusade, a sound like steel grating against steel slipped through the darkness. It was not the noise of any natural thing, and immediately my hackles rose. I peered in its direction and dipped into a defensive crouch. The sparse moonlight shone through the split in the clouds and illuminated the night just enough, allowing me to see through the thick rushes and to the road.

Six men stood there. They wore dark leathers and carried curved swords. One held a lantern and flashed its light in all directions. One crouched near my tracks and felt the earth. The others stood around him, peering into the darkness. Their voices I could not hear, unless I listened close. Then, they were but muted sounds in the distance.

They were fools. The lantern would destroy their night sight and give away their position, and their voices carried for long distances in the dark. Men such as these would not surprise much. Still, they may have been fools, but there were six of them. I was sorely outnumbered. If they found me and came on me at once, there was no way I could best them.

No way, that is, unless I took the shite-eaters one at a time.

I crept into the woods, circling to the right, keeping my eyes on my enemies when I could. Just as I had expected, they split. Two angled toward where I waited, two up the center, and two to the right. Unfortunately, it wasn't one at a time, but I figured I could take two. I predicted their route as well as I could and slid behind a thicket of ferns and rushes.

These assassins weren't nearly as silent as the last I'd faced. They were sloppy and ill-suited for stealthy killing. Their booted feet sloshed across the wet ground, and I smelled their sword-oil before they reached me. The ferns trembled as they moved. If there were but two or three, they'd perish easily. But there were six of them to one of me. If a single thing went their way, I was dead. I would have to be perfect in my craft. And, as Rayfe would have said when we still rode together, I was never, ever perfect.

I had intentionally stayed in heavy brush bordering a high, flat spot, empty of thick vegetation, thinking these men would take the easy route, and to give myself room to use my broadsword. I was not disappointed when the first two stepped out of the tall grass. They stayed close to each other for mutual support like line infantry. They stared ahead, intent on their expectant target, and not observing their flanks. It would be their downfall.

I let them pass and slinked from the brush behind them, staying as silent as I might. The first one died easily with my long-knife slipping across his throat. The second assassin cried out a blood-curdling scream and spun to face me. He was unprepared for my sword slamming into his arm and dropping his sword-side hand to a useless appendage. He turned to run, and I cut him down, my sword tearing through his spine and sending his headless corpse into the soft turf.

Their friends were now alerted, and I had no idea where they were. I headed toward their last known spot and began my stalk. They were easy to find, stumbling in the dark, struggling with the bulls-eye lantern. They were in the process of dowsing the light when I came upon them. I dispatched them easily, the first with a dagger into his back, and the second when he tried to respond. I drove my sword through his ribs.

I turned and moved toward the third pair. Again, it did not take long before I happened upon one of them. He waited for me, all bravado and folly, his weapon at the ready. He came at me hard from the front. I knew his partner was somewhere, probably behind me. These two were better than the rest. They'd flanked me somehow, and I didn't see a way out of it. I could not effectively fight them both at once. One of them would die, that was a truth.

I lunged forward, meeting his charge and feinting with my broadsword. As we closed, I changed tactics, switching rapidly and sweeping his sword aside with my long-knife, driving him forward and past me, and allowing me a glancing blow across his shoulders with my sword. It sliced through the leather and tore into flesh—a shallow wound. It was a move designed to degrade his confidence and turn me to face both him and his ally, whom I assumed was behind me at the tie.

But when I'd turned, his ally was nowhere to be seen. He came in again. I was off balance as I scanned for his compatriot, so I barely recovered enough to knock his blade aside.

He shouldered into me. He was a big man, and I was pushed backward, my breath knocked out of me. It was crude but effective. I let myself fall as his second strike descended. It sliced over my head as I rolled. I went arse-over-head and rose in a crouch, facing him. I lunged with my knife and slipped it across his upper arm, laying open the bone and rendering it useless. He cried out, and I spun sideways, avoiding an awkward swing, and chopped my heavy broadsword into his throat. He fell to the earth like a lump of shite.

I was exhausted, and I collapsed to a knee to catch my breath. I knew the dead man's partner was nearby, but my lungs were on fire, and my arms and shoulders burned. I needed a breath or two to collect myself.

I peered into the darkness as I crouched over the man, wary of attack. The corpse stared at me, and I rolled him over so I wouldn't have to look at his dead eyes. I sucked in air, my heart pounding. I tried to stay as quiet as I could, but I was afraid of failing.

The faint whisper of feet echoed behind me. I rotated my head and saw nothing. I forced myself to my feet and crept toward the noise. This fight would be hard, as I was near to collapse. But I'd be damned if I'd let the shite-eater take me without so much as feeling my steel.

In the end, it didn't matter how tired I was. I had barely taken a step from my resting spot before I discovered the body of the last man's partner. He lay on his back, his throat cut. His dead eyes stared into the night, and I instinctively looked away. I shook off a brief feeling of regret. His death explained why he had failed to kill me.

But who had killed him?

I heard footsteps disappearing into the distance. I moved as silently as I could, intent on pursuing this new player in my on-going drama. He was close, and he was very good. It was only chance that I'd heard him. I increased my pace, since I knew the stalker was aware of my location. I crashed through underbrush, running as fast as my exhausted legs and lungs would take me. Slamming through the willowing ferns, I broke into a small clearing and saw a figure on the far side, moving quickly.

I called out, "Stop!"

An empty face inside another dark hood looked back at me. It was too dark to discern much, but this one was dressed like the others. I surmised he was the same sort of assassin, cleaning up loose ends on a failed mark. I drew up and threw my knife, but he rolled under it, and my blade disappeared into the darkness. He followed it into the night, and I followed after him.

I may have been tired, and I may have been foolish, but I was faster due to my damn-it-all rush. I came upon him, and this time I emerged from the thick cover. I swung my sword sloppy and hard, and he easily parried. I realized too late the stupidity of my action as the assassins own sword hammered into my studded chest armor and sent me flopping onto the ground, blowing what remaining wind I had out of my lungs.

Just like that, my end was upon me.

The villain landed next to me after a graceful leap. He slipped a dagger against my throat. I stretched my head and bared my neck for him, waiting once again for death.

It was becoming an all-too common situation.

CHAPTER 10
ACCEPTANCE OF DEATH

I n war, there is a certain acceptance of death that one must reach in order to do what must be done. I had reached it long ago. During my last war, survival was my singular purpose—to escape the Crusade and return home to my family. When faced with the prospect of sacrificing my honor for my survival, however, I had gone against my instincts and chosen honor. I realized later my mistake. My honor had been lost years before when I had taken up the mantle of the Dark Men. My decision resulted in murder and a deeper plunge into depravity.

After returning home, I came to find that death also has a certain attraction to it. It is, I suppose, the end of the struggle. No more would I feel the hate and horror and self-loathing of the waking world.

At that moment, there on the rain-soaked ground with a knife at my throat, I looked up at my killer filled with acceptance. I had fought the fight, tried, without success, to restore my honor and find some sort of Absolution with The God. But I had failed. Perhaps these were impossible goals—in life, I concluded, there is little more than death and struggle. Sometimes the struggle is too much.

My killer drew up tall, a dark, avenging angel towering over me. He exhaled loudly and threw back his enshrouding hood. As it fell, I gasped in shock. I stared into a face I had hoped to never see again.

The apostate whom I had killed last year, the woman who had haunted my dreams from her grave, gazed down at me. Her eyes glowed with an unnatural blue fire. They bored into me, and a wicked smile crept across her face. My heart leaped into my throat and beat in a mad, pounding staccato. She pressed her curved dagger against my gullet. Its razor-blade cut lightly through my skin. I turned my head in an attempt to avoid her convicting gaze. I could barely think, barely breathe; the reality of what was happening was too intense. I had killed this woman, seen her life's blood drain from her, and felt her heart stop. I had seen her face a hundred times since. A spike of fear sliced through me and my breath caught hard in my throat. Was she a phantom, a vampyr?

I stammered, "You . . . are . . . a . . . ghost. A demon." I caught my breath finally, and added, "I saw you die."

"Yes you did. I *am* a ghost. But rest assured, I am no demon."

"By The God," I cried. "End it. End your cursed haunting. Take my life. I failed you, and you have risen for vengeance." I broke down, a year's worth of guilt overflowing and crashing over me. I sobbed and waited for death.

She stood up and off of me. "I have no wish to kill you, Aaron." She loomed above me in her dark leathers, her dirty-straw hair pulled back from her painted-black face. Her blue eyes glittered in the night. She was still beautiful, even in her war paint.

I sobbed again and felt a great weight descend on me. "How—"

"Later. We have no time," she said, her eyes focusing on some distant point.

She fixed on something other than our conversation, as if fighting some compulsion within her. I considered rushing her and killing her then. But the moment was gone before I could act.

"Your assassins are not Gols. These ones at least," she said at length.

"What are you talking about?" I stood and picked up my weapons, sheathing them. I could scarcely believe that I was talking to this manifestation of my guilt, this dead creature. Half of me wished to think I was in some sort of dream, some nightmare from a tale. It came to me then, like a shot. "You are the undefeatable warrior of whom the Bishop spoke." I had forgotten that part of the conversation because the Duke had dismissed it so quickly. Never would

I have thought such a thing. Never could I have imagined.

She ignored me, acknowledging my claim for a moment with a simple, "Perhaps."

But what did it matter? I faced her now, and the Bishop's demands to defeat her were lost in a swirl of fear, emotion, and curiosity. She strode to one of the corpses and, using the tip of her curved sword, flipped it. She stripped away its mask.

It was obvious once I looked at them. This one had red hair and green eyes—a dead giveaway for a northerner. In the mask and hood, it had been impossible to tell. I turned away from the face, its flat eyes and open mouth, where it was said the soul escaped.

"Their fighting style was also from the north," she added.

I had noticed it during the fight, but I had not made the connection. They fought like soldiers of the City Watch—competent, I suppose in a conventional way, but not like assassins. Whoever had staged this hadn't thought it through, or had expected it to be a simple affair. For these six, it had been anything but simple. They had paid with their lives. Who would have condoned such a thing? My immediate thought was the Knight Commander. The man hated me and judged me poorly at every turn. But, he was not the kind of man to kill in the dead of night, nor send assassins to do his bidding. Had I misjudged his zealotry for hypocrisy?

"You are still being followed by your own, you know," she stated. She turned toward me. I could not help but look away.

"I think you lie," I said, though I was not convinced after what I had just seen. I was tired, and my spirit was broken. I was still recovering from the knowledge that Edweene still lived, if indeed this was living. I needed some leverage over her, some small bastion of strength. I still saw those dying eyes when I looked upon her. She frightened me—rather, the thought of what she represented terrified me.

Lurking in my mind was the unsettling realization that my own side in this damnable war would send assassins after me. I didn't like not knowing who stood beside me and whom I could trust.

Could I trust anyone? I had to remain strong in the face of this haunted thing.

"I have seen no indication of being followed by more than these." I gestured at the fallen. "If I am being pursued, who follows?"

"Passage Knights," she said, using the slang for the organization of knights used by the common soldier. "At least twenty. Some miles behind. A half-day perhaps. They hang back, so as not to be seen."

"That is too far to be following. Perhaps they are only patrolling as knights are likely to do."

"You know better." She laughed. "You lie to yourself. The Holy Passage does not ride this far west. This territory belongs to the Knights of the Star. It is well known. Besides, I have seen your interaction with their Knight Commander. In the courtyard at the Holy City. You are not friends."

What she said of Gavreaux was true. Somehow she'd been spying within the keep itself. Did she have spies within? But, if it was true—that she was a ghost—perhaps it was possible she had witnessed it herself.

I drove away those terrifying thoughts. I chose not to acknowledge the comment about the Knight Commander at all.

"Territories of patrol are not known by me," I lied. I knew the truth of where the knights patrolled. The Star watched the Holy City and parts south and west. The Knights of the Holy Passage protected travelers from Golish raids on the Pilgrim's Approach and parts east of Clurak. That had been the way of it for years, unless things had changed since last I'd been in the Holy Land, which was unlikely. The Knight Companies were fiercely territorial about their responsibilities—worse perhaps than nobles.

I tried again to establish her identity. "They—those that sent me on this fool's errand—spoke of a cursed warrior who would not die, who fought like the vengeful dead. I suppose that was you."

She ignored me again, her blue eyes flashing. "I have been watching you."

"The raven," I said. "You are the raven."

"Not exactly, but let us say yes."

"Why have you followed me like this? Haunted my dreams, my every waking moment?"

"I told them you were weak, that they could turn you, that you would be more valuable even than I, for you have their trust. You are their Savior."

The idea that I was lured here by the heathen, that I was part of some scheme, seemed far-fetched. I was but a warrior. And weak? I chafed at the comment. I had killed her after all, not the other way around. "I am not weak. I have killed the best of them."

"I know you are not weak, Aaron," she said, almost apologetically. "The truth is I needed you. I need you to free me. To send me home. It was the only way to get you here, to get my masters to allow you to come—the only one that I trusted, such that I am able to trust."

"There is no way. Death is the only reprieve for the dead. Besides, I am a Crusader on a Holy undertaking of The God."

She winced from the comment and scoffed. "I know your heart, Aaron. You trust not in The God. You trust not in anything but survival. Your love for your sister makes you who you are. Your desire to make her believe in you. Our missions are aligned you and I." She gestured between us. "You must kill our general. I must be freed to go home."

"Home is not what you make of it," I whispered, almost silent. "It is not the same. More accurately, you will not be the same. I saw your sister. She hurts for you. I told her you were dead, your soul sent to Heaven."

She looked solemnly into the darkness. "She loves me and grieves. I have watched her. It is better that she thinks me dead, than what I have become. But you do not understand."

"Enlighten me," I said, emphasizing the last word. When she winced I regretted it immediately, and my heart softened.

"Death is the only reprieve for the dead," she repeated my earlier words.

I realized then what she meant—what she'd meant all those months ago. "You wish for me to kill you? Again? I cannot do this thing." Those eyes haunted me for all those years, how was I to suffer them again?

"Not again," she said. "For the first time. I saw it in your eyes that night, a year ago. Mercy. Not pity. That is why I sought you."

How am I to serve an . . . an . . . abomination?" I almost couldn't think the last word. Abomination—surely one risen from the dead would qualify. The Temple would say so. But I felt somehow responsible for what stood before me. I squatted and sat on the mushy ground. I pulled my knees close to my chest and stared into the night. I wished rest for her. I wished the silence of death to comfort her. But could I do it?

"If I were to help with such a thing—" I began.

"Kah Fau—he is a Necromancer. He raised me a lych," she said as though it was nothing. "The Gol horde thinks him a mere Sorcerer. But they only see what they wish to see. A death-wizard is an abomination to them. But he helps bring victory, so they chose to ignore his sacrilege."

She gazed at me sadly, those icy eyes suddenly soft and desperate. I recoiled in horror. I looked upon one of the walking dead, a lych.

Seeing my reaction, her eyes flashed hard again. She pulled away and added, "He holds my immortal soul. He has my soul trapped, Aaron. I may not die, while he yet holds it."

I could not even attempt to hide the horror. I coughed and looked at the ground. She was beautiful and so full of life. How could she be a lych?

"Did I make you this way?" I asked.

"Yes," she said, and I cringed. She must have seen it in my face, for she quickly added, "And no. You slew me that night, Aaron. But the Necromancer did this to me. He did it long before we met. He took me when my pilgrimage was massacred."

"And where does he keep your . . . uh . . ."

"Soul," she completed for me. "I am trapped in a phylactery embedded in a ring that he wears. I will lead you into their stronghold if you will free me, so I may go home."

"Why don't you kill him? You are capable enough?"

"I cannot harm him while he holds me. It is difficult enough to keep his mind at bay as we talk here tonight. He hears my thoughts when he is awake or focused. His power is stronger when we are closer. He can compel me, control me through his mind—rather his will—through his control of my soul."

"Then he knows we are talking now?"

"He sleeps."

"He sleeps? And you know this?"

"I believe he is sleeping."

"You believe? Do you always know when he is probing your mind?"

"Mostly. But not always. He can sometimes keep it from me."

I stepped away from her, staring into the night. My heart was cursed. I felt a strange attraction, an obligation to this lovely, dead thing. Was it love? Compassion? Empathy? All of these things? I knew not what. But could I trust her? By her own admission, this Necromancer controlled her thoughts and actions. And my own allies had tried to kill me. She had not lied about that. It was clear in the bodies that lay before me. Was there a purpose for my mission at all?

I turned to face her, my heart aching to help her, tears welling in my eyes. I was resolved in my decision.

"I cannot do this," I said after taking a deep breath and steeling myself.

She fell to the ground and shrieked.

CHAPTER 11
NECROMANCER'S CONTROL

E dweene rolled on the ground, her body convulsing and twisting in agony, clasping her hands to her head, her cries piercing the night like a dying creature. The pain must have subsided for a moment, for she paused, struggled to her knees, and locked my eyes with hers. She mouthed something to me, something I could not readily comprehend.

"It hurts," she howled and grasped her hands against her temples, nails digging into her own flesh so much that blood slid across her face.

I went to her and fell to my knees. I wanted to help, wanted to relieve the pain, wanted to do something. I grasped her body and pulled her to me, rocking back and forth as she panted and gasped. Her eyes flashed, their ice turned to fire.

She pushed me away. "Get gone. He comes for me. He comes for me. You can't be here."

I tried to hold her, but she shoved at me. Then she drew her knife and made to slash at me. In obvious agony, her slash was poorly aimed and went wide. I stepped back and stared at her, incredulous.

"Just go," she pleaded. "Please."

I had no options. She didn't want my help and was prepared to kill me if I stayed.

"Who is coming?" I asked.

"Kah Fau. The necromancer."

I nodded grimly. I would leave, but I wouldn't be far. I wanted to see this Sorcerer first hand, witness his black majyk, and understand what could turn the terrifying warrior who had defeated me on more than one occasion into the figure that now groveled in front of me like a broken thing. I stepped back and nodded, then jogged into the woods. Out of sight, I turned and quietly made my way back to deep brushy grass where I could see her again. I crouched and waited.

She hadn't yet recovered from whatever was causing her pain. She lay on the ground, moaning and holding her head. Her eyes were closed, and she was forcibly breathing in deep, steady inhalations—a focusing technique taught to many soldiers to deal with pain or fear or both.

I waited silently, settling into a comfortable position and careful not to let my eyes rest on her. One can sense when they are being watched, so I surveyed the surroundings, searching for anything out of the ordinary, any would-be enemy that might be hiding in the shadows. From the distance we were from the Golish camp, I figured it would be at least two hours until the sorcerer arrived.

After some time, she sat in a cross-legged position. She rested her sword across her legs, relaxed, and closed her eyes. As far as I knew, she had not discovered me. That was good, for if the Sorcerer could truly read her thoughts then I was safer this way. We were all safer this way.

It didn't take two hours for my enemy to appear. He arrived with surprising little fanfare, but his presence filled the air with heavy foreboding. A wave of pitch-like darkness presaged his arrival, sliding over the earth like a layer of oil on the sea. He followed not long after, a specter, floating above the ground and flanked by two great, hound-like beasts the likes of which I had never before witnessed. He wore a once-fine gray cloak that appeared burned and tattered. It was belted at the waist with a heavy black leather belt, laden with pouches. Glass bottles of various colors hung from it and glowed strangely in the night—red, green, yellow, and white. A curved dirk hung there too, its pommel a silver skull with red stones as eyes.

I could not see his face from where I hid, but on his head rested a brass or golden skull cap that glittered in the tiny light thrown out by the liquids at his belt. A strange sort of ghostly groan heralded him. My nose wrinkled when he passed near me. He smelled like day-old death. A dark fear permeated and rolled off of his being like a fog. I resisted the urge to flee.

"Edweene," he said as he stopped near her. His voice was hollow and full of menace. His two hounds flanked him, their jaws open, teeth gleaming. Spittle leaked onto the ground from their slavering maws.

She opened her eyes and glared at him. "Fay," she spit. I admired her fire. I wondered if I could face this creature with such courage.

He loomed like some kind of goblin from legend over a child it was about to steal. Slowly, deliberately, he removed the glove from his right hand, one finger at a time, and tucked it into his belt. Her face twisted in revulsion as he reached toward her with his bare hand. His fingers traced her face. A blue ring flashed on his fore-finger when he touched her.

She recoiled, the skin on her face rippling outward from where his skin made contact with hers. Tiny black fingers of rot crept across her cheek. Utter pain heaved over her expression, and her eyes flared with rage and hate. She opened her mouth as if to scream, but no sound broke the stillness.

His hounds danced nervously, licking their chops and glaring at her with undisguised hunger. I winced, my fingers tightening on my sword. I fought the urge to rush out and attack this madman.

"My beautiful little Nun," he said. "You cannot defy me."

"I would never," she mumbled as drool and blood dripped from her mouth to the ground.

He clenched his fist, and she startled, quieted, and fell to the ground, sobbing gently.

"Do not lie to me, my pretty one," he said. "If you could, you would kill me in a moment. Luckily for me, you cannot."

"I belong to you, my master," she forced through clenched teeth.

"Yes you do. I am pleased you realize that." He laughed. "Now, I know you dream of escape. But that is a fool's notion. I also know you have spared the knight from whoever was fool enough to attack him against my wishes."

"It was the Ek Inir's men. He fears this assassin," she said, her voice weak as she struggled against some unseen agony.

He clenched his fist again, and she squirmed and groveled. She doubled over and vomited onto the ground, black and green bile that smoked and sizzled as it soaked into the earth. Rivulets of blood leaked from her ears, and she fell into her own muck. She groaned and cried out, her scream echoing through the woods. The dogs jumped. They circled, sensing some sort of finale that would result in their feeding.

"The Ek Inir is a fool. This assassin is of much use to us. And I believe you know where he is."

"I am not lying," she said, spitting the words through clenched teeth. Her strength of will amazed me.

"Very well," he said, apparently satisfied. "Find him. Bring him to me soon, my sweet. You have always wanted a friend. Perhaps he can join you in your servitude. You two can share . . . things, stories and reminiscences of life." He laughed again, as though his grotesque jest was somehow funny. He squeezed his fist together one last time.

The Nun wailed, and the hounds howled.

"Your time is running out, dearie." Then, just as he'd arrived, he floated away, back toward his encampment, his hounds and his vile darkness receding with him.

When he was gone, I pushed aside the brush and stepped into the clearing. I settled over her inert form and gently stroked her head. Blood leaked from her nose and eyes. Bruises rose across a black and gray face that appeared to be half-rotted, skin peeling to reveal bone and flesh. I almost gagged when I looked on her, but swallowed it out of respect. Her eyes rolled up and focused on me. I smiled as well as I could after seeing that horror. I brushed sweat-soaked hair from her face.

"I am all right," she said. She clearly wasn't.

"Time will heal this," I said, but I wasn't so sure. I had witnessed much death in my young life, but I'd seen nothing as evil as this.

She laughed. "Understatement." She hacked frothy, blackish-putrid blood over her lips. "Hold me a bit," she whispered. "I will heal." She passed out, there in my arms, blood and vomit and bile soaking into my pants and jerkin.

I did just that, sitting there in that wet, flat spot outside the Torak Redoubt. I held the dead thing that I had grown to love and prayed to The God, whom I did not believe in, that she would survive. I started to sob as I cradled her for the second time in my life. And after I prayed, I forced away the tears.

I cursed The God for allowing such a thing, and I swore to the night that, for what I had just witnessed, I was going to kill that shite-eating savage. And then I'd kill his general. And then, I would move on, and I would butcher whichever turncoat bastard back at Clurak had tried to kill me.

I would kill them all or die in the pursuit of my singular goal.

CHAPTER 12
A VOW OF VENGEANCE

At some point, killing for honor and killing for a cause invariably become exchanged for killing in vengeance. In war, people die. And we think only those on the other side should die. When our friends are killed or savaged by some terrible thing, we find ourselves seeking revenge on those that committed the deed. Such is the cycle of war. It is not enough to defeat them, not enough to drive them from some territory, but we must exact vengeance for some terrible deed the enemy perpetrated upon us—the same one we likely inflicted upon them in the near past.

I was about to exact that vengeance. I cared little for the rightness of it. There should be rules in war. Certain things should be off limits, lines we do not cross. And the evil, dark, and shite-eating Necromancer had destroyed that line.

I held Edweene all night and most of the next day, not knowing how to help her. But she healed quickly. Wounds I thought to be mortal closed. She rose as the sun began its decline on the following day. She smiled at me, her eyes bright, skin whole and healthy.

"Does he know I was here with you all night?" I asked.

"I think not," she said. "He can see what I see and feel what I feel when he concentrates, but I have been unconscious this whole time. I've felt nothing. I've seen nothing."

"But now you see me."

She smiled. "Yes, I do. But the sun still graces the sky. He is likely asleep." She inclined her head and, it seemed to me, meant to kiss me. I leaned in, hoping to feel the softness of her lips, but she pulled away at the last minute. I let loose a disappointed sigh.

"I cannot," she said. "I am no real woman, Aaron. You know this. You said it yourself. I am a creature. A lych. I would not have you soil yourself thusly. Naught but darkness can come from our pairing."

I leaned back and let her head down slowly. Was she right? I did not know just then, but I held the same belief. The God would label her a demon or worse and demand her destruction. I wanted to kiss her more than I had wanted anything in a long time. But her fears were justified. What would come of that union, if even just a kiss? I backed away from her.

"We kill him," I said. "I am sneaking in tonight. And I am going to kill that dark bastard."

She laughed. "That was not your answer last night," she said, rubbing her hands against her cheek as if to massage life back into them.

"It is now."

We rose an hour later and made our way toward the encampment. We left my horse a half-league out and walked the rest of the way. It was nearly nightfall, and rain had once again began to drizzle, shading the dusk as dark as night. We strode up the road, as if we owned the land. I went before her; my arms were secured behind my back with rope designed so I could easily shuck the knots if we were attacked. She kept my sword and long-knife in her belt. I kept my dagger in my boot and hoped I wouldn't need it.

Two Golish guards rushed to meet us, their spears held at the ready. Upon seeing my captor, they fell back, making some strange circular motion with their hands over their hearts.

"They fear me, too," she said. "Just as you do. To them, I am dead—a vampyr or something worse. Whatever the case, I am the dead awake, and they will have nothing to do with me."

I let things go quiet. I had nothing to say, and this was her burden to bear. I understood it though. She was hated by all, an outcast, ever on the fringe, even from those for whom she fought and killed.

"We must be silent with our business," I whispered as we continued.

"Perhaps not," she responded. "Kah Fau has wards that encapsulate his home in silence, so the General and others do not hear the dark majyk he plies."

"Perhaps," I said, but I had better things to do than believe in such things. I would work as quietly as I might, despite these wards.

Edweene knew the path. As we made our way through the winding tracks toward the center of camp, Golish soldiers gawked at us, each of them giving way when she turned her eyes toward them. None had the strength to meet that gaze.

It was full night, when at last we reached the central tents. After passing through the guards and makeshift battlement that encircled the camp headquarters, we headed toward the great green pavilion with the serpent banner hanging limp in the dead, wet air. She stopped near the tent, and gestured to the guards. One of them grunted, turned, and went in—presumably to announce us. He came out and held open the tent flaps without so much as a glance at my captor.

When we entered, an isolated, trapped feeling overtook me as the majyk wards snapped shut around us. No one would hear our dirty business. The inside of the Sorcerer's pavilion was enormous, at least as large as my apartment in Rivershire.

The necromancer looked much the same as he had last night. He sat upon a tall, high-backed chair, which looked much like a throne, except it was crafted of blackened chitter-wood—a dark hardwood that was indigenous to Gol Toran and said to be imbued with the souls of those that died beneath its branches. The story was shite, of course. We tended to make up terrible lies about anything that originated from the vast Golish nations, so unknown were they to us. Still, witnessing the bastard and his black majyk last night added a certain credence to the old tales.

Kah Fau sat up in his chair as we entered. In his left hand he held a silver goblet, decorated with multi-hued gemstones.

Now that I saw his face, I was glad I hadn't last night. The Sorcerer was terrifying, having a visage that was perfect for his chosen profession.

Harsh, skeletal angles and sharpened teeth were set in a wickedly curved mouth. His hell hounds lay beside him, flanking the chair. Their long black tongues lolled between dagger-like teeth. They whined and looked up at him expectantly. His right hand lazily scratched at one's scraggly head.

"Master," Edweene said, choking on the word. "I have brought your prisoner. The knight, Ser Aaron of Rivershire, Savior of the Holy City." She tossed my weapons in front of me on the ground.

He rose from his seat, strode forward, struck an imposing pose, and stared at me. His eyes burned a strange, luminescent red-pink color, glowing in the near-darkness of the room.

"That you have, lych," he said, enunciating the word *lych* as if to disgrace and humiliate her. "As I knew you would, despite your childish insolence. In the end, you are mine. I hold your soul, after all."

I heard rustling behind me as she bowed or curtseyed or some shite like that. I swallowed a lump in my throat. I gave him my grimmest look and narrowed my eyes. It was easy; the hate was already there.

As if in response to my defiance, a wave of fear pushed from him and washed over me. I felt the urge to flee, but drawing on reserves of courage handily provided to me by my hate for the bastard, I somehow found the strength to stand my ground. I am sure, however, that the terror was evident in my eyes. I worked the knot that bound my hands. Freeing them had suddenly become imperative.

His face twisted in what was supposed to be a smile, but it looked to me like a growling beast. He held his right hand toward me, fingers outstretched. The lump of the ring protruded beneath his black gloves. I shuddered as something dark rolled off him. Edweene grunted, and I heard her knee hit the ground. He laughed—giggled like a child—and released his hand.

"Have you lain with her, Crusader?" he asked, his voice filled with sadistic glee.

I ignored the question. "Are you prepared to die, Sorcerer?" I advanced carefully into the room. My weapons were only a pace away. I could have them and be on him in a breath. I weighed my chances. They looked good from where I was standing, unless there was something about this sad, sick shite-eater that I didn't know.

"I have . . ." he said and smiled a sharp-toothed, maniacal grin

I remained quiet, sickened.

". . . lain with her, I mean. There is nothing greater than taking a woman's mind and heart, and then taking her body without her permission, even if she is dead." He cackled aloud, then.

"You are a devil, Ser," I said. "And you will pay for that defilement and all the others you have committed. You will pay with your life. I will send your soul into the Pit."

"You never had my heart, cur," Edweene shouted. She rushed toward him, spinning as she passed me, her curved sword raised above her, ready to sever his head from his shoulders.

"No!" I hollered—so much for silence. But it was too late. She was already past. She was faster than me. She always had been.

The hounds rose to a guard position. He stepped back between them, then howled at her, "No. You will not attack me, whore!"

She slowed her rush involuntarily, like a marionette being pulled in a puppet theater. And then she stopped, standing dazed in the center of the chamber. Her sword fell from her grasp, landing on the carpet-covered floor.

Enraged, I rushed forward, diving into a roll to grab weapons.

The hounds lunged at me. The first fell easily, my broadsword piercing its throat. It had expected no fight from me and died for its stupidity. The second was not so impulsive and circled me. The monster lunged as I struggled to pull my sword free of the first. Realizing the blade was stuck too deep, I turned too late to stop the beast's attack, and it latched onto my leg with its massive jaw.

"Kill yourself, nun," the Necromancer's voice boomed through the tent as I struggled with his beasts. "Drive your sword through your own heart. You will know who is master here, and I will no longer accept your impudence. I will kill you and raise you again and again and again, until you understand."

Involuntarily I screamed as the beast worked on my leg like a bone, shaking its head from side to side. My vision faded, and I almost passed out from the pain, but I pushed away the darkness, drawing on all reserves of strength and willpower I had remaining. I struck at the hound with my long-knife. The blade bit into the flesh on top of its skull, parted the pelt and muscle there, but didn't penetrate the rock-like bone. The beast on my leg shook harder, unwilling to release me. It dragged me toward the throne.

Behind the creature that dragged me, I caught a glimpse of Kah Fau. He screamed in rage, his eyes glowing intensely. He raised his chalice high above his head, its contents steaming and bubbling. Lances of orange flame shot down his arm and torso to blast through his right fist, which was pointed directly at Edweene. The flames stormed from his fingertips, arching the small distance between them and engulfing her. Fire consumed her. She was flung backward to land in a corner with a *thud* that shook the tent above us.

I could do nothing for her until I was able to defeat the dogs. Using the foot that was not locked in the creature's jaws, I kicked my boot into its face, tearing away part of its nose and spraying blood across the Necromancer's chair. But it was to no avail.

The creature stopped and, for a fragment of a moment, released me to get a better grip.

I took advantage, yanked my leg free from his jaws, and simultaneously thrust forward, hard and fast with the knife. The point of the blade dug into the thing's cheek, the bone directing the blade upward and into its eye. I rammed with full force when I felt the softness of the eye give way. The blade plunged into its brain. With a loud gasp and a high-pitched whimper, the creature slumped and died.

The Necromancer laughed out loud and cried, "Today you die, and tomorrow you die again."

He renewed his assault on Edweene as she staggered under the onslaught. Waves of flames rolled from his hand, through the dark room, and over her body. She shrieked, falling to her knees, as her flesh and clothing burned. The scent of scorched hair filled the room. She pushed herself up, lunging a few tiny steps before falling to her knees again.

Worried that she might be killed any second, I managed to yank my broadsword from the first beast and launch myself at the Necromancer.

I thrust my sword before me as I charged, my damaged leg sending stabs of pain through my hips and back. My scream drew his attention, but it also alerted him to my attack. He lurched, letting the flames die. But he was not quite fast enough, and my blade dug into his guts, driving through his lower torso as easy as butter. He staggered. The smell of bowel and piss filled the room. He raised his hand and fire lashed toward Edweene.

"Die," he cried.

I swung my sword in a great, overhead arch that brought the razor edge down upon his arm, severing the appendage and sending it spinning across the room.

He snapped his head toward me and cried out in pain. Crimson blood pumped from his arm and from the massive tear in his gut. He stumbled backward, disbelief in his eyes and fell into his chair. Somehow, he'd held onto his goblet, and he spilled the fizzing, smoking contents over himself and his chair.

The air swirled darkly for a moment, and the dying Necromancer, Kah Fau, disappeared into nothing.

CHAPTER 13

KILLING THE GENERAL

Kah Fau's bloody hand lay upon the floor, severed just below the elbow. He had fled the combat through whatever black majyk gateway he'd summoned. But he would die soon. He had lost so much blood, and his bowel had leaked like a sieve. There was no surviving the kind of wounds I had inflicted upon him. He would perish in terrible pain. I felt grimly satisfied at that.

I stepped over the corpse of one of the hounds, careful of the pressure I put on my wounded leg and picked up the severed hand. I removed the glove and gazed upon the ring. It glowed brightly, its blue aura shimmering around the inner chamber of the tent, illuminating all manner of dark things.

Edweene looked at me, fear in her eyes. She was crawling from the corner. Her left cheek was burned away and melted; much of the blackened bone beneath was visible. I had to look away, unwilling to see the damage that Kah Fau had inflicted.

With this ring, I could step into the Necromancer's shoes, control her like the marionette he had tried to make her. I knew it. She knew it.

But there were limits to this power—the wearer must have the strength of will to control the lych. I held the thing between thumb and forefinger and showed it to her. My thoughts were that she had me beat in the willpower category. She smiled, uncomfortably.

I was not him. I would not control another like he had, whether she as lych or not, whether I had the strength or not. Humanity was not in the blood. Humanity was found in one's actions, anxieties, feelings and fears and conscience. Edweene was as human as I and deserved her freedom.

I glanced at her, fighting the urge to avert my eyes from her pain, and tossed her the ring.

Edweene held the tiny piece of jewelry and stared at her phylactery, wonder etched on her fire-damaged face. The crystal glowed with renewed light, illuminating her face in brilliant shades of azure. Her eyes shone with the same intensity as the stone. So too did her smile, white teeth against blackened flesh—it was perhaps the only true smile I'd seen from her, as macabre as it was.

She stood and extended her fingers. The Necromancer's hand was considerably bigger than hers, but when she slid the ring down her finger, it adjusted to size perfectly. She smiled again widely and picked up her sword.

"It is time to kill your general," she said.

"Yes," I responded, clapping her on the shoulder. "Yes, it is."

The General's tent was only a few paces from the necromancer's, making our infiltration easier than we could have hoped. The majyk wards around Kah Fau's pavilion had protected us from prying ears, so we did not worry whether the guards or the general himself had heard our murder. I considered slicing my way through the side of the canvas but was warned by Edweene.

"The Ek Inir has it warded. An alarm would sound and pierce the night like a banshee's shriek."

So we decided against it. We would kill the guards up front and infiltrate through that entrance.

It was a dark night. Clouds hid the moon and guaranteed there would be no light to give us away. Only sound was our enemy. And we were helped in that regard as well. The rain continued in a steady drizzle, softening our footsteps and clouding the ears of our enemies. We sliced a gash and slipped out the back, careful to avoid tie ropes and stakes.

Two guards were posted outside of the great tent. A lantern was suspended from a looped iron pole nearby. The light was perfectly situated between the guards and us. Their night vision would be ruined by its flickering orange glow. I watched the ground, so the light would not do the same to my eyes. They stood, confident and inattentive, fearing nothing this deep inside camp.

I turned to whisper a plan to my companion, but she had already moved. She raced quickly toward the closest guard, barely a smudge in the darkness. When she struck, it was fast and deadly—her blade sliding across the man's throat before he had time to react. He gurgled once and slid into her waiting arms. She caught him and lowered his body to the ground.

The far guard heard the noise and turned, raising a horn to his lips. Instinctively, I loosed my long-knife at him. At this range, missing was nearly impossible, and the blade tore through his eye socket. He collapsed to the ground, his mail crashing as he impacted. I cursed Edweene's impetuous attack, worried that someone would have heard.

My fears were well founded. Unbeknownst to us, a third guard stood inside the flap. He flung open the doorway, his long, two-handed falchion greeting us first. The big man didn't have a chance to react.

Edweene was unnaturally fast, and before he even realized there was someone outside, her sword had already severed his throat. Red blood sprayed across her charred face as she swept into the giant pavilion. I followed her in, stepping over the corpse and pulling my knife from the eye of my victim as I passed.

The inside of the tent was one large, open space divided by a single row of canvas sheets. The first section was a war room. Scattered over the floor were scores of fanciful pillows. A large, low table squatted in the center. Atop the table, numerous maps and scrolls laid. Candles burned. It was still relatively dark, but the candles lit the room in a yellowish, flickering haze. It gave the feeling of hell-on-earth.

To our right, a large, wooden obelisk—an altar to the Old Gods—stood, a mouth at its base containing some sort of meat as a sacrifice. To the left, a large, padded chair rested, its reddish leather seat worn from too much use. Sconces of sweet smelling incense burned in the four corners of the room. Directly across from us, another threshold was marked with a slit in the tapestry. We listened and heard nothing. Parting the slit ever-so-slightly, Edweene slid her head in and peeked. A moment that felt like an hour later, she withdrew and smiled at me. I grimaced and tried to smile back as well as I could.

"All's quiet. Some wine. Some fornication. And our general is ready to die," she whispered almost gleefully. She stepped through the slit, and I followed after.

When it comes down to it, even the greatest among us—generals, and kings and heroes—are the same, frail, vulnerable creatures as the lowliest of us.

The great general, who had confounded the soon-to-be Holy Defender, thrown down one of the Knuckles, and inspired a Fourth Crusade, lay sleeping before us on a large padded floor-cushion that was covered in colorful pillows and silk sheets. He was nearly naked, entwined in the arms of two lovely and nude Golish women, their long hair splayed around him like a dark halo.

I nearly averted my gaze, so shamed was I at the scene. It seemed almost wrong to kill a man in such a way. There was something unpleasant about murdering a naked man, about destroying a warrior with this man's repute for handling a blade and for leading an army, while his manhood hung for the world to see and an unknowing smile—no doubt from a night of merry-making—was drawn in unmistakable pleasure.

"He's yours," she whispered. In her voice was challenge, as if she could sense the indecision in my heart.

"I am not a murderer," I whispered to myself.

There was mirth in her blue eyes. It was oddly disturbing, such obvious delight at my damn-fool comment, set upon the blackened visage of her skull-face right then.

"Yes, you are, Aaron," she whispered. "You have been since you walked the Pilgrim's Approach, on the last Crusade. There is no shame. It is who you are."

I gazed at her, dumbfounded and surprised at her wisdom. Then I looked to my target and sighed. I nodded. I slid my sword into its scabbard and slipped my long-knife from its sheath.

"Now do it, so we can be gone from this place," she hissed.

I leaned over him, stiff-legged and in pain, placed my hand over the man's mouth and pushed the knife under his chin and into his brain. His dark eyes flew open, wide with the realization that his mortality was near. I looked away from his face, unable to meet his eyes as life fluttered out of him. He thrashed once, twice, and expired silently on the cushion.

I wiped the knife's blade on my sleeve and returned it to its sheath. The women slept.

My mission was accomplished. It seemed at that moment to be so meager, so pitiful that this was the culmination of so much effort—that the silent murder of one so powerful could be done so easily in the end. In my heart though, I had done something irreparable. I had fallen deeper into some pit I could not yet identify.

I started to retreat, to leave the scene of this despicable act, when Edweene leaned over one of the women and made to slide her dagger

across the concubine's throat. Reacting as quickly as I could, I stayed her hand before the blade
bit flesh.

I shook my head. Edweene gave me an implor-
ing glare, and I returned the sternest gaze I could.
I would have none of that. My soul was stained
enough.

Blood pooled beneath the General's body and
pumped over the sleeping girls. I did not wait
for Edweene's answer and fled toward the door.
I couldn't stop her if she decided to kill the girls,
but I would not witness it.

I slipped from the tent, exiting the way we had
come and careful to step over the bodies of the
dead. In seconds, Edweene joined me.

We retraced our steps. The path was wet-
ter, and rain was falling in earnest. We stepped
quickly, but not so much as to arouse suspicion.
In the darkness, obscured by the rain, we might
be mistaken for soldiers of Gol—if all went well.

Unfortunately, it never does for me.

We had reached the halfway mark when a terrible scream pierced the night.

"We should have killed the girls," Edweene said simply and started running.

I ran after, knowing she was right. A horn blew behind us, too close by far. It was followed by shouts of, "The General's dead. They have killed the Il Aruk!"

"Hurry, man," she called to me, surging ahead with a demon's speed.

"Damn, I am running, woman!" I called back, unable to keep up, the wound in my leg sending pain racing over my entire body. "Damn The God, I am running!"

She slowed a bit, and I flushed with embarrassment. A Gol stepped from the darkness next to her, and I impaled him on my blade. She nodded her thanks, and we continued our flight.

Arrows slipped in and out of the night around us, swishing sounds that embodied invisible death. I staggered as one struck my leg, scarcely cutting through my leather greaves and penetrating the surface of my skin. A second arrow slid across my studded breastplate and spun into the dark. I yanked the shaft from my leg, flung it to the ground, and continued my mad escape.

Ahead, the gateway loomed.

CHAPTER 14
ESCAPE

E scape is largely a function of luck when an assassination goes sour. This assassination had definitely gone sour.

I found myself running like a madman through an enemy camp, dodging arrows and hoping—for skill was pretty much impossible at this point—for survival. Edweene was ahead of me, probably gloating about the correctness of her desire to kill the two women. I had chosen mercy.

Another lesson for me: in the business of murder, it's important to leave behind predilections for such things as mercy and honor. They have no place when holding a knife at someone's throat. Those are the things with which I struggled. But that was for another time. Like I said, right then, I was simply trying to survive.

We ran harder, the sounds of pursuers directly behind and to the sides of us. Two guards stepped up to meet us at the gate—the same ones we'd passed earlier. They lowered their spears to receive our charge. Exchanging glances between themselves, I could see the fear in their eyes reflected in their lantern light. I sped toward them.

Edweene was on my left now, sprinting. She was ahead of me by a body length. The guard to our left pivoted to face the lych, his spear planted in the ground and shaking in unsteady hands as he clearly contemplated his fate. I moved farther to the right, still staying on the path but wanting to split the defenders. Everything happened in a matter of breaths, and before the guards could truly be prepared for us, we were on them.

Edweene dived feet first toward the man-at-arms, while sweeping her sword arm up to knock away his weapon, meaning to slip under his spear point. He could not react quickly enough to deal with her attack, and she slid easily under his defense. She knocked the shaft of his spear with her curved sword, pressing him back, as she came on with her dagger. He tried to swing his spear, but she was too close for such a long weapon, and it bounced harmlessly off her shoulder. In short order, her dagger was in his neck, and he fell upon the makeshift battlement behind him. I watched as she leaped over the spiked barricade while I faced my defender.

"Hurry on, man!" she cried from the other side. "They come from our flanks, too."

Sure enough, outside the battlements, a column of Golish cavalry rode toward her through the night. Their torches bounced and shuddered as they came, illuminating the bearded faces and silvery spears. They were long moments away, however, and I had my hands full. I was not as fast as she was, but I was quick in my own right. And my leather armor was considerably lighter than this man's scale hauberk.

Setting for a charge was a defense designed to deal with lines of on-coming enemies and was difficult to employ against a singular foe. I had to give the man tribute for standing his ground, but he had probably chosen the wrong maneuver. As I rushed him, I changed direction a breath before I was upon him. I shifted left, spinning with my sword in a wide arch. He could not match the move and found his spear woefully out of place.

My weapon landed on his shoulders, but the force was not there. It slammed into his armor and deflected wide. But I felt the crunch of bone. He grunted in pain but spun toward me, stepping backward to free up his longer weapon. Knowing I had to keep inside of his reach, I stepped in quickly, dropping my knife and grabbing ahold of the shaft of his weapon. He tried to jerk it away from me, but I was the stronger, and I had leverage. I yanked him toward me.

Recognition flashed in his eyes as he realized that he was done. I glanced away from his face as I thrust my sword into his gut. The steel ground into his armor. I pressed with all my strength, felt it slide through, slipping into the flesh beneath and out the back where it stopped, having insufficient force to punch through the armor fully. He gasped and collapsed to his knees. Avoiding his dying eyes, I released the spear, wrenched my sword from his body, grabbed my knife where it lay on the ground, and vaulted the makeshift rampart.

It all seemed for naught. We had escaped the camp, but twenty knights of the Golish army bore down on us, merely moments away. Edweene grabbed my arm and pushed me onto the road.

"I will hold them," Edweene said. "Go on. Get to your horse. Escape!"

I was so filled with the anxiety of war that I ran a few steps down the road, not thinking of the implications. When her sacrifice dawned on me, I turned toward her. She faced our would-be killers, her curved sword held at her side.

The lead men spurred their horses and rushed, lances lowered. She would die there in that charge, lych or not. They would likely burn her body to ash afterward—there would be no coming back from this.

I considered running my life for hers. She had volunteered it. I could reach my steed and be gone. So simple a thing. I even started to turn, my last vision of her being a valiant stand against a cavalry charge.

I stopped my flight. How could I do such a thing?

I had watched her die once, left her for dead. I would not do it again. I had abandoned honor once. I would claim a little back right here. We would die together.

"No!" I called and rushed to her side.

I arrived just as they reached us. She cast me an angry glare and leaped sideways, dodging the first lance and driving her blade into the breast of the lead horse. The poor creature died almost instantly, its momentum carrying it arse-over-head into the brush beside the road. The rider went with it, grunting as he slammed into the ground.

I, too, dodged to the side, but I was not so lucky. My rider's lance crashed, a glancing shot into my side that sent me spinning. The wind was knocked out of me, and I felt the busted bones in my ribcage. A gash had been torn in armor, a long split through the treated leather.

Through a haze, I watched as they closed in around Edweene. She would be dead soon. I dragged air into my lungs with a gasp and, with great effort, forced myself to my feet. I picked up my sword and staggered across the road toward the battle. Another spear slashed into my thigh, sending me once again to the ground. Blood poured over me, coating my lower torso and legs in a hot, sticky mess.

"Edweene," I called and caught her flashing blue eyes as she skewered one of her attackers and dodged yet another. But there were too many of them, and she staggered as a sword crashed over her shoulder and sent her reeling backward a few steps. She surged into the fight and cast me a devil's grin.

Yes. We would die here together. The thought was sobering but not at all uncomfortable.

I grasped one last time for my fallen sword and pushed myself to my knees. I was too far gone; my strength had left me. I tottered and fell.

I watched as she was overwhelmed by a rush of cavalry. She disappeared into the melee as horses' legs suddenly surrounded me. I knew I was done. I held up my hands and cried, "Take me, you damn heathens; I have killed your general."

A horn blew, and a whistle sounded. I heard the crash of steel on steel, followed by grunts and shouts. I was grabbed by my arms and yanked up by strong hands.

"Up, man," a familiar voice called. "I will not let you die here!"

I looked into the face of Knight Commander Gavreaux. He smiled broadly at me, his visor pulled up so I could see his eyes. They were filled with concern and determination. I had never been so glad to see someone who hated me.

"Ser Telor, help him up."

Another set of strong hands pushed me onto the back of Ser Gavreaux's steed. I grabbed the knight around the waist, leaning my head against his back. I had no strength to ride high in the saddle.

"Sound the withdrawal," Gavreaux called. A horn blew, a whistle sounded, and we fled into the night.

CHAPTER 15
THE RAVEN'S GAZE

The King's coronation occurred the night before I awoke from near-death. I had been invited, but my wounds precluded my attendance. The northern kingdoms crowned our first Holy Defender, King of the Holy Land—the once Duke Lethan of Greenshire. Greenshire now belonged to his son Soren, a cruel little man who was once the Earl of Crowe. Soren of Greenshire was now my liege, and I wondered what that meant for my small holding.

So much can change in the blink of an eye or the slash of a dagger. I rose and shuffled to my window. Set on the northern tower, my apartment overlooked the Sea of Sorrow. Right now, I saw anything but sorrow. The celebration continued despite the overcast skies and dark thunder-heads that rolled our way.

The war was not yet over. Murdering the Ek Inir had only delayed the inevitable. The heathen army had withdrawn to determine a new leader. It seemed they had the same infighting among nobles as we. I supposed it was the nature of men to seek power. But they would come again, and they would be angry and hard.

To the east, the Crusade had begun to arrive, my captain, Ser Willem, with them. Deprived initially of a fight with the heathens, many of the Crusaders set up encampments outside the city walls. Soldiers, supply trains, and camp followers had become a nuisance. Thievery and rape and whores would be commonplace.

One cannot contain an army such as that for long. I hoped Willem would have the mind to avoid the madness. But the nobles among the Crusaders, primarily led by Trok, Crown Prince of Rogga, were already chafing for a fight. Soon, they would have it.

I stepped out of my apartment and was met by Knight Commander Gavreaux at the door.

"Good morning, my lord," I said and bowed my head in greeting.

"Good morning, Ser Aaron," he responded. "I am off to The Stone. I must reunite with my Order. I have been chastised—and appropriately so—for leading my knights on land sworn to the Tears." He referred to the Knights of the Tears—the knights sworn to protect the Holy City and the western expanses.

"The Stone," I repeated. "It is a cold, hard place."

"That it is. But it is my place. The intrigue here is too much for a simple knight of the cloth."

"When I am better, I shall seek you out. I must find the man who betrayed me." I owed him and meant to repay. I also needed his help if I were to continue my quest, my oath.

He looked at me and frowned, tilting his head. "Aaron, I wish you would not. I have nothing for you."

He laughed, and I laughed in return. Then he turned and strode down the hall away from me.

I re-entered my room and poured myself a cup of red wine. I stood by the window, peering out to the Sea of Sorrows and wondering where events would take me next. Far to the north, I heard the call of my family's home—my sister, asking for me to return. And I felt the longing in my own heart.

According to her last letter, my sister was courting some lordling from a nearby Thayne-hold. I'd be lying if I didn't feel like interrogating the man or threatening him with bodily damage. But things in the Holy Land didn't feel finished. Indeed, things were definitely not finished. My Crusade had only just begun. I would find my betrayer.

There was still killing to be done.

Outside, I watched as bowmen and artillery-men walked a silent vigil on the battlements, manning the cold, never-used batteries meant to guard against sea attack. Their war, quiet and uneventful until now, was about to get very real and very bloody very soon. Death drifted on the wind.

A raven perched on a far tower, its blue eyes staring in my direction. I stood tall, looked in its direction, and toasted her with a tip of my cup. Somehow, she had escaped. I imagined her fleeing into the woods under the cover of the Crusader charge.

"Here's to you, Lady Edweene," I said and then, after a moment of thought, added, "and to those haunting blue eyes that have troubled all my nights. You have saved me once again."